MW01146811

Keri's Christmas Wish

Pamela S Thibodeaux

"For unto us a child is born, unto us a son is given: and the government shall be upon his shoulder: and his name shall be called Wonderful, Counsellor, The mighty God, The everlasting Father, The Prince of Peace." ~
Isaiah 9:6

KERI'S CHRISTMAS WISH
by
Pamela S Thibodeaux

Publisher/Distributor:
Temperance Publishing; an imprint of
Pamela S. Thibodeaux Enterprises, LLC
PO Box 324, Iowa, LA 70647

Copyright © 2016 by Pamela S. Thibodeaux
ISBN# 978-1539596769

Cover Design: Get Covers

Published in the Unites States of America
Publishing History: First edition Dec. 3, 2016

Note:

This novel is a work of fiction. Names, characters, places and incidents are either the product of the author's imagination, or, if real, used fictitiously. No part of this book may be reproduced or transmitted in any form or by an electronic or mechanical means, including photocopying, recording or by any information storage and retrieval system, without the express written permission of the publisher, except where permitted by law. The scanning, uploading, and distribution of this book via the Internet or via any other means without the permission of the publisher is illegal and punishable by law. Please purchase only authorized print and/or electronic editions, and do not participate in or encourage electronic piracy of copyrighted materials.

Your support of the author's rights is greatly appreciated.

Praise for Pamela S Thibodeaux

"Pamela Thibodeaux uses her masterful story writing art to create a powerful story of how God heals a woman's heart —broken by grief— through recovery, love and triumph." ~ CBA Best-Selling Author DiAnn Mills on **My Heart Weeps**.

"A great collection of short stories. Each one includes inspirational romance. Wonderful choice when you need a quick pick-me-up. I have not been one to read short stories. This book has changed that. There are times when they are the perfect choice." ~ (Amazon) Review of **Love in Season** by K. Neely

"Loved this book. Wish everyone could read this. Definitely puts all holidays in perspective. If we remember the reason for the holidays then we must put God first.......always. I will certainly recommend this book. Great stuff keep up the great writing." ~ (Amazon) Review of **Keri's Christmas Wish** by Reba

"Oh, the passion, faith and just LIFE that flows through this book...powerful writing indeed!" ~ Review of **Circles of Fate** by Deena Peterson, Book Reviewer @ A Peek at my Bookshelf and Just One More

"Thibodeaux leads the reader through from the first page to the last without once relinquishing control. She hooks them, holds them, and keeps them enthralled until the last line." ~ Review of **The Visionary** by Delia Latham

"Through Pamela's blessed ability to find God everywhere, even in secular song lyrics, she has written devotions guaranteed to touch the heart and remind the reader of our True Love, the Rose of Sharon." ~ Endorsement for **Love is a Rose** by Linda Yezak, Author, Editor Triple Edge Critique Service

"**In His Sight** caught my attention from the beginning and it made me wonder if I had given all to God as he gave all to me. Thank you, Pamela for a story that I would readily recommend to anyone who needs that extra encouragement!" ~ Reviewed by Wendy for Happily Ever After Reviews.

*"**Winter Madness** is a wonderful romance and an excellent example of Spiritual growth."* ~Reviewed by Dee Daily for The Romance Studio

*"**A Hero for Jessica is** a good, sweet read charged with attraction but an emphasis on true love. I recommend it to women of all ages."* ~ Reviewed by Violet for LASR

*"**Cathy's Angel** is a short tale that is entertaining as well as inspiring. Well done!"* ~ Reviewed by Marlene for Fallen Angel Reviews

*"Pamela S. Thibodeaux's motto is "Inspirational with an Edge!" Her short story **Choices** lives up to those words and is well worth reading."* ~Reviewed by Gail for Night Owl Romance

*"**The Inheritance** was my first Thibodeaux work; however, it will not be my last! Her approach to writing about everyday life, while struggling to maintain strict Christian standards and values, is a glimpse into reality which we all must face from time to time."* ~ Reviewed by Brenda Talley for The Romance Studio

*"If you have ever considered Christian fiction bland, then check out the **Tempered Series**. It will be well worth your time."* ~ Amanda Killgore ~ for Huntress Reviews

*"**Lori's Redemption** is fast paced, lots of action, gripping storyline... I loved it. It's gone straight back into my TBR pile."* ~ Clare Revell author of "Monday's Child" series

Dedication

All **Thanks** belong to God for the glorious gift He has entrusted me with – the gift of writing that enables me to share my faith and His love with the world!

To Delia, critique partner, and friend – You constantly amaze me. Thanks for **ALL** you do!

Special **Thanks** to all of the authors, writers, poets, and artists who have paved the way for me to do what I love and whose work I admire – *Thank you, Thank You, Thank you!*

Last but certainly not least, Pat Sonnier ~ my beloved **Mama**...you left us too soon. Love and miss you always.

Thank You, Dear Reader.....

I pray you are as blessed as I am by your purchase of this book. If you've enjoyed **Keri's**

Christmas Wish, please write a positive review, and post it at online retailers (Amazon, B&N, Kobo, iBooks, etc.) and websites where readers gather and/or your social media platforms (FaceBook, Good Reads, BookBub, Twitter, etc).

Chapter One

Bah humbug! Keri frowned as she scrolled the news feeds on her social media sites. *The madness has started already.* Christmas in July. Before long it'd be Christmas decorations up alongside Halloween costumes and Christmas stockings next to turkey stuffing.

The entire world went bug-eyed crazy when it came to Christmas.

"What are you grumbling about?" Jeremy looked up from his tablet. *Oops.* The crease in his forehead indicated his confusion, and no wonder. In the six weeks they'd dated, not once had Keri given any indication to her aversion to the holiday season.

Oh, well, he's bound to find out soon enough.

Irritation crawled up her spine and leapt through her lips. "We've barely gotten past

9

Independence Day and now everyone is jumping on the 'Christmas in July' bandwagon. Aggravates the fire out of me."

"What have you got against Christmas?"

"Nothing, except it's a false holiday."

"Seriously?"

Was that curiosity or dismay in his expression? Probably both, poor guy.

"Yeah. I mean, according to every theologian I've read, studied under, or debated with, Jesus was not born on December 25th. He wasn't even born in December. And, even if he were, this holiday has become anything but a celebration of His birth.

"It's an overinflated season, hyped up to rip off the public with ridiculous schemes and price gouging in order to get more money for something of little or no value. Then, when it's all over, the retail industry moans and complains about how much money they 'lost' until I want to puke up tinsel, lights and icicles."

Jeremy ogled her as though she'd lost her mind. "Wow, not sure if I want to know what made you so cynical."

She took a deep breath and tried to find an answer—as much for herself as for Jeremy. She couldn't recall any particular incident that turned her against Christmas, but her aversion for the holiday went way back in her psyche. Had she ever not been a bit of a Christmas scrooge?

Keri shut down the computer and stretched a kink out of her shoulders. Crossing the room to where he sat reading, she slipped her arms around Jeremy and gave him as cheerful a smile as she could muster. "I'll get over it. Maybe this will be the year of my Christmas miracle and I won't feel this way anymore."

He eyed her, one eyebrow arched in question.

"I've prayed for years to understand these intense feelings I have about the commercialism of Christmas, but so far, no such luck. I don't know when it all started or why, but it's been my wish for years that I could just chill and enjoy the festivities."

He squeezed her in a tight hug and kissed the tip of her nose. "Then that's my Christmas wish for you also. I'll add it to my prayer list, and we'll see what happens. In the meantime, I'd suggest you stay away from sites that promote the 'Christmas in July' propaganda and find ways to start looking forward to the real celebrations."

She smiled up at him, this time for real. "Will do. Now what are we doing for dinner?"

Jeremy glanced at their attire and suggested a familiar, classy-but-casual diner. Keri ran a brush through her sable hair, and they were out the door. Conversation remained sweet and lightly romantic while they ate, and

Christmas wasn't mentioned again until they were almost home.

"What kind of things have you done besides prayer to uncover the root of your Christmas malady?" Jeremy shot her a quick smile before returning his attention to the road.

Keri shrugged. "I've read every cute, funny, serious and spiritual story around the holiday, watched sweet and humorous movies, sat for long moments of silence in front of nativity scenes and brightly decorated trees and tried to figure it out. I just can't seem to get past the commercialization into the heart of the issue."

Jeremy pulled into a spot next to her car, put his in park and turned to face her. "Well, I'd be willing to help you. If you don't think that would be too weird or anything."

She pressed a kiss to his cheek and opened her car door. "I don't think it'd be weird. I'm just afraid you might run as fast and far as you can away from me when you find out how truly crazy I am." She tried to laugh as she scrambled from the car, but the sound lacked even the tiniest trace of humor.

Jeremy hurried to catch up and walked with her to the door of her apartment. He turned her in his arms and pressed a kiss to her lips, then took her key and opened the door. He didn't walk away until she closed and locked it.

Keri smiled as his footsteps faded into the night. As always, Jeremy made her feel safe and protected. Not too common in men these days, but she liked it a lot.

Jeremy made his way back to his vehicle, the echo of fear in Keri's words striking a nerve deep in his heart.

Keri Jackson was highly intelligent, deeply emotional, and intensely complex. He'd known that the first time he saw her. As a psychotherapist, he'd dealt with personalities as diverse and varied as the different species of plants and animals which inhabited the earth. The fact that he encouraged the use of spiritual practices with his patients made his treatment unique, if a bit unorthodox from a medical standpoint.

Jeremy believed God was much bigger than man could even comprehend. The study of religious modalities and how they played into the human psyche fascinated him. That's why, when a patient shared their personal beliefs with him, he was able to incorporate those beliefs into a highly specific, individual program, along with modern techniques and methods of accessing the deepest level of consciousness in that patient.

At home, Jeremy changed into sweatpants and a T-shirt and settled in for his nightly devotions. With a Bible, prayer journal and pen in hand, he added Keri's Christmas wish to his prayer list, and then had a conversation with God.

* * * * *

Keri lay awake for long hours after Jeremy dropped her off. "Oh, Lord, what would You have me do? I love you with my whole heart. Why can't I get past this issue with Your birth?"

The musical tinkle of wind chimes filled the air. Keri closed her eyes and listened as the sweet melody soothed her troubled spirit. Soon she drifted into a dreamless slumber. When she awoke, sunlight streamed through her bedroom windows.

She pushed the covers back and swung her legs over the edge of the bed while her mind went through the litany of things she had to be grateful for. She'd implemented this practice years ago. It stirred up enough positive energy to get her through the snarl of morning traffic and safely to her office across town where she immersed herself in the demands of her accounting job.

During her lunch break, she thought about the previous evening, and Jeremy's discovery of her sour outlook on Christmas. Only then did she remember hearing wind chimes as she drifted off to sleep. Where had the sound come from? She didn't have much time to ponder the question.

Noontime aerobics and a quick shower before hurrying through her usual fare of sandwich, yogurt and fruit took up most of her concentration. She made a quick mental note to check the neighboring apartment decks and balconies to see if she could find the source of the heavenly strain.

Later that evening, Keri sat in her apartment bewildered and confused. Her search around the apartment complex after work had uncovered not a single string of wind chimes. Not one. She'd found nothing to explain the music she'd heard while drifting off after her evening prayer the night before.

Goose bumps rose on her flesh in response to the shiver that shook her soul. Could it be God used the music to acknowledge her prayer? Would this be the year she finally let go of all the angst she felt around Christmas and just enjoyed one of the holiest seasons? Would her Christmas wish finally be granted?

The ring of her cell phone startled her so much she nearly jumped out of the chair. She picked it up, noted the caller and pushed the button to answer. "Hello."

Jeremy's voice came through the speaker. "Hey, how was your day?"

"Fine. Busy as usual. We're getting our mid-year tax clients so that keeps things interesting."

"Mid year?"

"Yeah, you know, those who file extensions in April in order to buy more time to get their records caught up? They usually start bringing in what we need to get organized so that we can file for them in October. All quarterly reports are due by the end of this month too."

"Oh. Ugh, I don't see how you do it. Numbers drive me crazy."

She laughed. "Ditto on what you do. I doubt I could listen to other people's problems without taking them upon myself. I'd go bonkers right along with them."

"It's a balancing act, for sure," Jeremy replied. "But when in a healing profession, you learn to take exceptional care of yourself– mentally, physically, emotionally, even spiritually. Those of us who believe, that is."

"Yeah, it's amazing how many more doctors are using their faith while practicing and are not afraid or ashamed to admit it."

A buzzing whine in the background made her grin. She pictured him in his kitchen, opening a can of something while they chatted.

"Medicine has come a long way in the last several years. Even psychology has changed."

He hesitated, popped the top on a can, drank, and swallowed. "Sorry, I know eating or drinking while on the phone is rude, but I guess I didn't get enough fluids in me after my run."

Keri laughed. "No problem. What do you mean, psychology has changed? In what way?"

She heard him pull a chair out from the table, then another, and sigh. From the sounds of movement, she imagined he'd stretched out and propped his feet up.

"What I mean is, with the discovery, or should I say rediscovery of energy medicine, and the mind, body connection—which is becoming more and more scientifically proven, as well as the body's natural means of healing itself, the whole scope of healthcare has changed. Even psychologists and psychotherapists are picking up on some of these energy-related techniques and are finding great progress with some of their most difficult patients."

"I've never heard of energy medicine," Keri remarked.

"It's fascinating. Might be a bit boring for someone who deals in numbers though." He chuckled.

Keri laughed. "Maybe, but I'd love to hear more about it."

"Well, we will have to get together over the weekend. I can show you a couple of books about it. So, what's new since I saw you last night? Which, by the way, I truly enjoyed."

His voice had softened a bit. Her heart did a slow swirl into her stomach. "So did I. Not much has changed, but something a little strange happened as I drifted off to sleep last night."

"What?"

Keri bit her lip, hesitant to tell him about the wind chimes.

"You can tell me anything, Keri. I promise not to make light of what you say."

I can't be any nuttier than some of his patients, she reasoned. "I said my normal evening prayers, and then, just as I dozed off, I heard the sound of wind chimes. At least, that's what it sounded like. This afternoon, I drove around the apartment complex to see if I could spot any on someone's porch or balcony, but I didn't see a single chime of any kind. Kinda freaky."

The same fear in her voice that tugged at his heart the night before, touched him again. Jeremy sent a silent prayer for guidance in helping her. He tuned in to his intuition. "I don't think it's freaky at all. Seems to me God had the angels hum you a lullaby."

"You know, I thought the exact same thing."

A warm, toasty feeling enveloped Jeremy at the excitement in her voice. "One thing I've learned while walking with the Lord is that He will answer us in the most unusual and amazing ways."

"You really do have faith in Him, don't you?" she asked.

Jeremy nodded, then realized she couldn't see him or hear his brains rattle. The thought brought a smile to his lips that echoed in his voice. "Yes, in ways most people find strange or radical. I believe God is much bigger than the boxes we put him in, especially those outlined in traditional religion."

Her soft sigh filled him with a joy he'd not experienced with any other woman.

"I believe that too. So much so that I usually feel out of place in church."

"That's because we tend to fear what other people think or might say about us if we let go and truly worship Him. But the Bible does state that God is a spirit, and we should worship Him in spirit and in truth."

"But whose truth?" The question had haunted Keri for a long time. "Every religion has something different. Every preacher you listen to teaches their own interpretation of the Bible. It can be so confusing."

"That's why it's important to spend time with God in prayer and meditation and to let Him show you the truth, His truth, as it applies to your life. We get so caught up in what one pastor preaches and another one teaches that we fail to go straight to the Source. Go to God, listen to Him.

"I'm not saying preachers and teachers aren't valuable. Just the opposite, but they should point us to a personal relationship with Him. And those are as unique as each individual human being."

His phone clicked. Jeremy glanced at the caller ID. "Hey sweetheart, I have to take this call. We'll talk again soon. OK?"

Keri agreed, and he switched over to accept the incoming call.

* * * * *

Keri put her phone down, enlightened and encouraged by her conversation with Jeremy. In all of her adult, and, if truth be known, her young adult years, she'd never met anyone who so easily expressed what he or she believed. Nor had she met anyone who appeared to be on a similar path as she—though she was sure Jeremy far surpassed her on the spiritual plane.

Many times, in her searching for truth, she'd heard faith teachers tout the value of meditation, but she'd yet to give the practice a try. Tonight, she wanted to, but had no clue on how or where to begin.

In a sudden burst of memory, she recalled a book she'd read, and the author's definition of 'practicing the presence of God.' She'd try it.

As she set about her nightly rituals of dinner, dishes, and bath, she kept God uppermost in her thoughts instead of allowing her mind to wander aimlessly as it usually did, circling on one worry after another. She began a dialogue with Him in her mind, then transitioned to speaking aloud words of praise, worship, and prayer.

"I don't really know what I'm doing, Lord, but I desire a more intimate relationship with You. I want to know You better, to hear Your voice, to recognize when You are speaking to me or showing me Your will, Your plan, and Your ways.

"I'm no longer happy relying completely on the experiences and teachings of others. I need to feel You myself, to experience Your fullness in my life. In all I think, in all I do, and in all I believe. I've been so caught up in learning *about* You, and I'm grateful for all I've learned and the many teachers who've taught me, but now, from the deepest parts of my heart and soul, I want to honestly *know* You."

As the evening wore on, her words became song and she once again drifted to sleep with the lovely melody of the night before ringing through her dreams.

Chapter Two

Saturday morning dawned bright and clear. Sun streamed through the windows as Keri flipped back the covers and exited her bed. The usual litany of gratitude poured from her heart. Words rushed forth from her lips and she literally sang aloud the list that played in her head until every cell in her body tingled with joy.

She had never felt so alive!

Each day she deliberately kept God first in her thoughts for the better part of every hour. When her attention wandered, she would take several deep breaths and bring her mind captive to Christ. Her daily breaks at work consisted of quiet time where she focused on God, Jesus, Holy Spirit, and the angels.

Songs of praise and worship from her years of religious upbringing evolved into refrains of her own design as she felt more and more connected to God. The wind chimes she'd heard that night nearly a week ago became a heavenly chorus which rang through her soul on an almost continual basis, and she couldn't wait to see Jeremy and share with him what she'd experienced this past week.

They were due to meet at the park in less than an hour.

In an effort to hurry herself along, Keri turned on the radio. Before she could change from her usual Country music station to a Christian one, a commercial blared about another 'Christmas in July' sale. Her heart sank as the same old frustration rose in her breast.

A low scream sounded in her throat. She threw back her head, curled her fists, and clenched her eyes closed as silent tears streamed down her cheeks. "Oh, God," she moaned. "I thought I was getting over this.

What was this week all about if not to get past it?"

Seething with disappointment and resentment, she slapped the 'off' button and finished her morning toiletry, and then left the apartment to drive across town. She didn't bother camouflaging her emotions as she pulled into the parking spot beside Jeremy's car and slammed out of her vehicle.

"What's wrong?" Concern etched every line of Jeremy's face and resonated in his voice. In answer, Keri threw herself into his arms and burst into tears.

"I d-don't k-know what I'm doing wrong!"

Jeremy ran his hands up and down her back in a soothing gesture and waited until her sobs subsided before he asked again. "What's bothering you, sweetheart?"

Keri scrubbed the heels of her hands down her face and accepted the handkerchief he held toward her. "It's just so frustrating."

He waited while she pulled her thoughts together.

"I was so excited to tell you about my fabulous week and then this morning that stupid commercial came on the radio again and the whole concept of spiritual growth blew up in my face."

Jeremy took her hand and began to walk along a path that led to the pond at the far end of the park. "OK, so tell me about your fabulous week."

"What good does it do now when the glory of it has fizzled into reality? I haven't changed on a deep enough level to end the aggravation I feel about Christmas."

He let go of her hand long enough to administer a soothing stroke down her back, then twined his fingers through hers again. "Telling me about it might bring back some of the excitement and splendor."

Keri took a deep breath and described her experiences over the last several days. As she did, the beauty, awe and wonder filled her heart again, battling the angst of the morning. "I just don't understand how I could have such incredible encounters all week and then lose it all in a single moment."

"You haven't lost it, Keri. You lit up while you shared the moments of connection you experienced over these past days. No sole incident can erase that. In my profession, you learn over and over that change takes time. Things may seem to improve on the surface, but soul deep conversion takes longer. Letting go of old mindsets, old beliefs and standards can be a continual process. Progress comes in stages."

"Kind of like one step forward, two steps back?"

He grimaced. "Some people look at it that way. I hate that analogy though because it makes it seem as if your progress is limited. I like to say that if you've held on to a certain belief for twenty or thirty years, give yourself at least that many months to enact complete transformation.

"Even when you feel you're no longer stuck in that particular mindset, certain circumstances may bring those old feelings and thoughts to the surface. That doesn't mean you have to start over, just that you have to remind yourself how far you've come, and that you've been delivered from those old thought forms. Then you can reinstate your new belief.

"More like salvation. Jesus saves us once. Period. Now the Bible tells us to continually work out our salvation, but what that means is to always be on alert for attacks of the enemy that fill you with judgment and condemnation, making you doubt you're saved at all. Or his lies that convince you to ask God over and again to save you. You don't pray for salvation every time you backslide into an old habit He has delivered you from, or fall from grace on an issue you thought you'd overcome, do you? You may ask Him for forgiveness and more grace, but you don't pray for salvation again."

Keri mulled over his explanation for a few minutes, letting the truth and comfort of his words fill her with hope and courage to keep practicing God's presence to the best of her ability in every moment of each day.

She turned to face him, took his hands in hers and stood on tiptoe to brush her lips across his. "Thank you. I'll bet you do wondrous work with your patients. You sure have made me feel better."

He caressed her cheek with the back of his hand. "I'm not the Healer, love, just the vessel. Not the Source of Wisdom, only the messenger."

Keri's insides turned to mush at his use of the term 'love' when addressing her. She smiled. "And you do both beautifully."

* * * * *

Journal and pen in hand, Jeremy reclined in his favorite chair. After the initial upset with Keri, the day had been wonderful. Thumbing through the pages, he recalled when he'd met Keri nearly two months ago, and the initial impressions he'd had as well as the opinions and intuitions he'd experienced since.

They'd both been waiting in line at the post office and struck up a conversation which continued outside in the parking lot and culminated with the exchange of phone numbers. He'd been so swept away by her that he started keeping a journal that very same day.

This technique, which he'd found effective in dealing with and understanding his patients, became something he maintained on other significant people in his life. Journaling enabled him to be more specific in his prayers, as well as his research and study of the human psyche for the books he hoped to write one day.

Nothing fascinated Jeremy more than the mind, body and emotions of man, and the effect one had on the other. How the mind could cause fear to manifest in the body and how emotions could influence both physiological and psychological functions amazed and baffled him in equal parts. When you added the spiritual aspect to the equations, it added a whole new level of intrigue to the entire concept of what a human being was comprised of. He'd found that miracles and madness sometimes went hand in hand.

Opening to a blank page, he prayed while recording the incident of the morning.

"Dear God, please help me to see through Your eyes, listen with Your ears and understand with Your divine intelligence and compassionate heart. I believe Keri is the woman You've ordained for me and if so, then my desire to help her has a two-fold purpose. If she is not, then I ask for Your wisdom and direction in channeling these feelings I have into their proper place in this relationship.

"Most of all, Lord, keep me humble in mind and heart. I don't want to allow my expertise and thirst for knowledge to become a block or a weapon, but a means through which Your divine love, peace, joy and harmony may help heal and lead Keri to wholeness in mind, body and spirit. Thank You. Amen."

Chapter Three

Keri lingered in bed, her mind replaying every moment of the day before. Never in a past relationship had she allowed herself to be as vulnerable as she'd been with Jeremy these last couple of weeks, especially yesterday. The fact that he was a psychotherapist might have something to do with how safe she felt in his presence.

She had felt somewhat safe in other relationships, only to have her idiosyncrasies thrown in her face when they ended. But something about Jeremy convinced her he was different. Maybe the kindness in his hazel eyes or the tenderness in his voice, and definitely the compassion he radiated in every circumstance.

"And that voice." She sighed, rolled over and smiled. He had the most incredible voice...all husky and breathless and.... rich. Like a hot toddy—warm milk laced with honey and a splash of whiskey.

Keri closed her eyes and recollected the resonance when he called her 'love.' Warm shivers danced along her spine and goosebumps rose on her flesh as heat pervaded her entire being.

She allowed herself a few moments to wallow in the feelings he evoked in her, then slid from beneath the covers, determined to take Jeremy's advice and continue her recent practice of being in the presence of God on an ongoing basis. She figured her desire for a more intimate relationship with Him would benefit her in many ways even if she didn't get to the bottom of her antipathy over the date of His birth.

She completed her morning ritual then picked up the journal Jeremy gave her yesterday. She thumbed through the scriptured pages, hearing his robust tone when he said how beneficial he found journaling to be.

"You may be surprised, Keri, at what you discover about yourself, your life and your faith by writing–thoughts, dreams, gratitude lists, goals–whatever comes through you onto the paper."

She prepared a cup of hot tea, turned on the radio and switched it to a Christian station, then grabbed a pen and curled up in her rocking chair. "OK, God, I've never done this before, but I believe Jeremey when he says it can be a powerful process for healing and self growth. I have no idea where to start, so I'm just going to write whatever comes to mind."

She took a deep breath and focused her heart and mind on Jesus and the Holy Spirit and put pen to paper.

An hour later she skimmed back over the pages, humbled and yes, amazed at what she'd written. Words of praise and thanksgiving, dreams long denied–some forgotten, whispers of what could only be God speaking to her deepest soul.

The clock chimed nine. Keri scrambled from the chair and hurried to dress and leave for church services which started at ten. She arrived with a few minutes to spare and found Jeremy pacing the sidewalk in front of the building's entrance.

"Sorry I'm late."

He touched her cheek then took her hand as they made their way through the door. "No problem. Everything OK?"

"I'll tell you about it later." She found herself speaking in a whisper, reluctant to spoil the tranquil atmosphere inside the cathedral.

The two found an empty pew moments before the choir director announced the opening hymn. Flipping to the proper page in the hymnbook they shared, they lifted their voices and joined in the praise and worship songs.

For the first time in a long while, Keri found herself acutely aware of every nuance of the service that morning. Upon leaving the building, she mentioned this to Jeremy.

Jeremy slid her hand through his arm and walked in the sultry morning air toward the café two blocks from the church. "When we begin to open ourselves to the true power and presence of God, we tend to experience things on a deeper level, especially those of a spiritual inclination, like church services, walks in nature, pieces of art, etcetera. God is so...."

He considered what word would be apt enough to describe the absolute hugeness of God. "Expansive. That's the best word I can come up with. He is so vast that when we look and feel things from an enlarged or enlightened viewpoint, through His eyes, ordinary life becomes extraordinary. Colors, sights and sounds are amplified to us here on earth as they reportedly are in heaven."

Keri narrowed her gaze. "Have you ever met anyone who claims to have been to heaven? You know a near death experience or anything?"

"I've had clients and personal experiences of God, Jesus, angels and heaven. Many in the medical profession would say those are hallucinations of the mind, stemming from a religious upbringing and/or practice, but I believe most, if not all, are valid to some degree. I mean, I know what I've experienced, so why should I doubt my patients' episodes?

"Now, that said, different degrees of mental illness can be partially to blame in some fears and phobias, but not everyone who encounters the beauty and tranquility of a heavenly happenstance is mentally incapacitated. Some

44

are actually quite sane and outside of these occurrences, live normal, healthy lives in every other area."

"Fascinating!"

Once seated in the cafe, they continued the conversation.

"So, are you going to tell me what happened this morning to have you run late?" Jeremy leaned forward and fixed his gaze on her.

She hesitated, fidgeted with the napkin on her lap.

Jeremy's discernment of body language and senses heightened. He reached over and took her hand, stopping the restless movements. "You don't *have* to tell me, sweetheart."

She smiled and his heart skipped a thud.

"I just don't know where to begin." She laughed, clearly uncomfortable. "This morning was so exquisite, but now everything seems surreal."

He smiled. "That's what they all say. But Keri, I know you. Pretty well, I might say, for the short time we've been dating. You are not flighty or eccentric. You're well-grounded and down to earth. So, whatever you tell me will not change my perception of who you are. Should you decide not to tell me anything at all, that's OK. I'll respect your privacy."

After the waitress took their orders, Keri picked up the conversation.

"I really love that about you, Jeremy. You're so...I don't know, *real*, I guess it's almost scary. We haven't even known each other two whole months, and yet, I feel as though I can be my true self around you. There's no need to pretend on any level to be anything I'm not."

She shook her head. "I know that sounds crazy, but with everyone I've ever dated, and with other people in my life, I've felt like I had to be on my 'best'"—She finger-quoted the word for emphasis— "Behavior at all times. I couldn't mess up in conversation or laugh at an inappropriate joke or too loud, especially in public, or even at a ridiculous scene in a movie.

"All of my life I've been corrected for actions which came naturally, and so I've built this persona around the real me. It's refreshing to feel so at ease around you—almost too good to be true. I guess I'm just waiting for the newness to wear off to see if you'll turn out like everybody else."

Jeremy chuckled. "I know what you mean. Ever since I was a young boy, I've felt and seen things and people differently. As a Christian we are called to look a level deeper. As a psychotherapist we're taught to do the same. But in the spiritual world, practicing this trait is known as being an empath."

Keri cocked her head, intrigue written all over her face. "I've never heard of that. I know what empathy means, but I've never heard someone referred to as an empath."

The waitress arrived with their food. After a few minutes of silent contemplation, followed by a prayer of grace and blessing, Jeremy took up the discussion where he'd left off.

"There's so much mystery, fear and anxiety around the psychic, or spiritual abilities human beings have, it's ridiculous. We scoff at things like intuition, except when it comes to a woman and her child. 'Mother's intuition' is accepted, but the truth is, we *all* have intuitive capacities. We're just not taught the value of them and how to use them for the overall enlightenment of mankind.

"Then, of course, so many horror novels and movies are built around these attributes of the human mind. And the teachings of early church leaders labeled it wrong and something to fear. We've strayed away from our natural, God-given means to connect more deeply with Him and His creations."

"His creations?"

"People, animals, plants, angels. Did you know angels are mentioned in the Bible more than one hundred seventy times? We're told God has given His angels charge over us, that they encamp about us, and are here for our protection and guidance. Yet most people refuse to believe when they hear a voice out of nowhere, or see a flash of light, color or shadow out of the corner of their eye, that it might be their guardian angel. The very word 'angel' means messenger of God."

A knot of food and emotion lodged in his throat when Keri's eyes lit up. A smile curved her lips, and Jeremy swallowed hard.

"I've felt the same way!" She emitted a tiny, self-conscious laugh. "This is just too awesome that we'd see angelic beings in the same light.

I've never met *anyone* who thinks about them the way I do, and I was beginning to think I was weird or something."

Jeremy chuckled. "Not at all, sweetheart. You're probably one of the more sensitive ones."

A frown creased her forehead. Keri put down her fork and covered her near empty plate. "Then why do I have this aversion to Christmas?"

Jeremy pondered her question a moment then reached over and took Keri's hand. "I don't think you're experiencing an aversion to Christmas itself, just the hype and commercialism around it. Could it be you're annoyed with that aspect because it takes away from the true meaning behind the holiday?"

"That's part of it," she admitted. "The rest stems from the rhetoric around the actual time of Jesus's birth, the different calendars... Jewish, Chinese, Western... all of it is just so confusing and frustrating. I'd love to know the *real* truth."

"Considering there are different types and levels of what people deem as 'truth,' that might cause even more confusion. Does it really matter the exact date of Jesus' birth, or is it more important that we authentically celebrate the Incarnation? But don't worry, we'll not only get to the root of your angst around Christmas, we'll dig it up and eradicate it from your heart, mind and spirit."

She rolled her eyes. "Now you're telling me there are levels of truth. That's all I need to hear."

This time Keri's laughter came from deep within and caused a resounding delight to leap within Jeremy's heart. He grinned.

"Ready to head out?" He signaled the waitress for the check.

Keri excused herself to the ladies room while he paid for their meal, then they walked back to the church where they'd left their cars.

Jeremy pulled her hand through his arm. "What do you have planned for the rest of today?"

She shrugged. "Nothing. You?"

"I had hoped we'd spend the afternoon together, then maybe have dinner."

"Sounds like fun. What would you like to do?"

"How about we go for a drive and see where we end up?"

"I like that idea." Keri slid into his vehicle when he held the door open for her. "I guess it won't hurt to leave my car here?"

"Not if we plan on being back in time for evening service. Either way I'm sure it'll be fine."

They headed south out of the city. First stop was to tour an antebellum home. They took selfies together in front of the humongous fireplaces and in the gazebo. Holding hands, they wandered through the luxurious gardens. Jeremy nuzzled her cheek when he overheard the elderly ladies behind them remark what a cute couple they made, then chuckled when Keri blushed.

Once the tour ended, Jeremy continued their journey to a nearby bird sanctuary.

"It's so hot," Keri remarked as they approached the concession stand.

"Yeah." Jeremy pulled her into the shade beneath the stand's canopy. "How about an ice cream cone?"

"That sounds wonderful."

They each picked a flavor and were soon overcome with laughter. The ice cream melted faster than they could eat.

Kari licked at the cool concoction, then giggled as the dripping mint chocolate chip oozed down the side of her hand to her wrist.

Jeremy laughed. "Guess this wasn't the best idea."

Keri tilted her head and tried in vain to stop the leak which sprung from the bottom of her cone, then doubled over laughing when Jeremy tried, also without success, to keep his top scoop from plopping onto the ground.

"What's so funny?" He faked a pout, then leaned over and kissed a stray chocolate chip from the side of her mouth.

At the surprised pleasure on her face, he tossed the cone aside and covered her mouth with his in a tender yet thorough gesture. Stepping out of her embrace, he eyed the mess her cone made on his shirt. "Nope, not the best idea today."

Keri looked down at the disaster they'd created. "Not appropriate for evening church services either."

Jeremy laughed. "Well, then I guess we have time to visit another wildlife park or something."

"I'd like to try and wash some of this off." A frown creased her forehead.

They went to the restrooms and met up again shortly, shirts damp from the quick attempt at damage control.

Hours later, the two said goodbye after a day filled with laughter, joy and discovery. Jeremy gave her a couple of energy medicine/psychology books and shared with her some self-help techniques. Keri determined to be open-minded enough to give them an honest try. He also suggested she prayerfully ask for specific guidance or messages.

"It's not rocket science." He tugged on a strand of her hair. "Nor is it sacrilegious as some would be quick to say. However, God won't usurp our free will, nor can the angels. But if you *ask*, expecting an answer, they will respond. I've even had patients write a question down in their journal, then close their eyes, meditate in silence, and just write what comes to mind. They're always surprised at what is revealed to them in this manner.

"Christians have practiced meditative prayer for centuries. The problem arises when we don't understand how to discern spirits, as the Bible tells us to do. We can open ourselves up to the wrong spirits and be unaware of having done so." He laughed. "I'm sorry, I'm starting to preach!"

He sobered. "Keri, if you try this, don't push for an answer to your dilemma over Christmas the first time out. Ask something simple yet direct. Ask for a clear, unmistakable sign in answer to your question, something only God would know, and you would recognize. And always pray for protection from the evil one so you won't be deceived. The devil can come as an angel of light, and it's not always easy to see him coming. It's why so many people—especially beginners—get caught up in spiritual things that are actually condemned by God for our wellbeing."

So once again that evening, Keri sat with diary and pen in hand, candles lit and music on low. She closed her eyes, took several deep breaths, and allowed her mind to empty of its chatter and focus on God.

"Father God, Jesus, Holy Spirit and angels, I'd like to thank You for Your presence in my life and the many blessings You've bestowed upon me. I'd really like to come up higher in my prayer life and spiritual walk. Protect my mind, heart, and soul from the influences of the devil and draw me closer only to You. I ask for a unique, identifiable sign that You've heard my prayer. Thank you and Amen."

When her mind began to wander, filling her brain with ceaseless chatter, she walked around a bit, then resumed her humble position and waited. The now-familiar sound of wind chimes filled the air. Electric pulses pricked her skin. Keri continued to pray in soft tones but kept her eyes closed and stayed put.

An image began to form in her mind...a young girl being led around on a horse by an ethereal figure. As the trio came closer, Keri felt as though she looked in a mirror. Her heart swelled. Tears clogged her throat, filled her eyes, and slipped down her cheeks.

"Hi, Keri!"

The childlike voice reverberated through her entire body. Keri smiled and whispered, "Hello."

Excitement lit the youngster's eyes. Brilliant colors vibrated around her. "Do you know who I am?"

"You're me as a little girl. That's Spark, my horse who died when I was a teenager."

Spark nodded his head as the girl giggled—a joyous melody that rang through the atmosphere. "No, silly, I'm your big sister. Only, I didn't live very long."

Tension seeped in, a mixture of shock and awe.

"Don't be afraid. Ask mom."

And then the mirage disappeared.

Keri opened her eyes and shivered. "Oh, God, is that the clear sign I asked for? My sister..."

Her words trailed off as Keri strove to write every detail of the vision. She knew her mom had miscarried before her own birth, but no one had ever said whether the child was a boy or girl. After she finished recording her experience, Keri called her mother.

"Hi, mom, how's everyone and everything over there?"

"We're fine, honey. How are you and that nice, young man you've told us about but we've yet to meet?"

Keri laughed at the teasing in her mother's voice. "We're good. I promise I'll bring him over to meet y'all soon. Hey, I have a question for you."

"And I've got an answer."

"I'm sorry if this brings up sad memories, Mom, but the baby you miscarried before I came along...were you far enough in the pregnancy to know the sex?"

"Yes, actually, she was a girl. Why do you ask?"

Keri hesitated. Her mom might not understand the apparition. She condensed the event into a version that at least *sounded* reasonable. "Just curious. While praying earlier a vision of a young girl popped into my mind and made me wonder."

"Oh...well, I guess we'll understand more when we get to heaven."

The kingdom of heaven is in your midst.

The scripture floated through her conscious, but Keri said nothing. They chatted a few more minutes, and she didn't mention her sister again.

Later, as she lay in bed, she said another prayer of thanks for the wonderful day with Jeremy, and the splendid things she'd experienced during her prayer time.

Chapter Four

Jeremy awoke the next morning filled with hope and expectation. His time with Keri the day before had evolved into a long evening of prayer and meditation. As a result, his personal spiritual growth took a leap into the deeper aspects of God. He loved it when that happened. When a remark or conversation or the mere act of guiding a friend, loved one, patient, or client resulted in a boost of faith for himself.

Which is exactly why he did what he did for a living.

He stretched long and deep then crawled from beneath the covers. The moment his feet hit the floor, he indulged in another luxurious stretch, then bent to make his bed. Next in his morning ritual was coffee. The aroma just now beginning to filter in from the kitchen filled his senses with delightful anticipation of that first cup, to be enjoyed during prayer and meditation, after which he'd shower, dress and be at his office in time for his first client.

Unease curled in the pit of his stomach. The woman due to meet with him at ten a.m. could prove to be one of his more difficult cases. He'd accepted her as a patient at the request of one of his colleagues. More like an appeal than request.

This doctor had seen her for years with no visible breakthrough. Why she'd assumed he could help when she herself had been unable to was a mystery, but Jeremy appreciated the vote of confidence. As his mind continued to circle around the upcoming appointment, he determined to stay in peace about the whole situation.

He poured a cup of coffee, settled in his meditation chair, and then quieted his mind. As he sipped the rich, dark brew, he wrote the thoughts and impressions which came to him in the journal he'd chosen for this client after studying the chart her prior doctor had provided. He headed out an hour later armed with a host of ideas and possible solutions.

Jeremy arrived at his office to find Ms. Jennah Anderson already there. He recognized her from a photo attached to the file his colleague had provided. The sheer desperation in her eyes sent indecision curling up his spine. He took a deep breath and offered his hand. "Hello, Ms. Anderson. Nice to meet you. I'm Dr. Hinton."

Tears filled her eyes. She reached out in return. "Dr. Hinton. Thank you for agreeing to see me."

The moment their hands touched, images of her from infancy through adulthood flashed through Jeremy's mind like a video. Emotions bombarded his spirit…. pain, shame, anger, loneliness, extreme sadness.

He released her hand with a slight curve of his lips. "I appreciate you being a tad early. Give me five minutes to chat with my receptionist, and I'll be ready to visit with you for a while."

She smiled but the effort did little to erase the darkness from her countenance. "I've all the time in the world and nowhere else to spend it."

He chuckled. "Haven't heard that phrase before. Angela will send you back in a few moments."

He moved into his office and, after a quick consult with Angela, spent a few minutes in silent contemplation. Only then did he signal for Ms. Anderson to come on back.

He waited while she settled, albeit uncomfortably, in the chair across from his desk before he spoke. "How can I help you?"

"I'm not sure you can. No one has been able to before."

"Why do you suppose that is, Jennah? May I call you Jennah or would you prefer Ms. Anderson?"

"Jennah is fine. I don't know why. I've spent the better part of my life speaking with various counselors and physicians, yet no one can give me a definitive answer as to what ails me. Between my primary care doctor and numerous psychologists, I've tried every drug in the book to help alleviate this depression, but nothing works."

"Tell me what else you've tried."

She frowned. "Like?"

"Group therapy, art therapy, hypnosis therapy, anything you would consider *did* help even a little?"

"No. I'm uncomfortable around strangers, I don't like crowds and I'm not about to let someone mess with my mind and have me behaving like some kind of animal or be so vulnerable they can convince me to perform some disgusting, perverted act."

"Those are mostly myths associated with hypnosis, Ms. Anderson. Although we *are* sensitive to suggestion, any doctor worth his or her salt would never use this tool for anything that would go against a patient's moral compass. More often than not, the patient themselves would snap out of hypnosis if something the doctor said went against their deepest convictions."

Her derisive snort assured him she wasn't convinced he could help her.

Jeremy scribbled notes and considered his next question with great care. "May I ask you a direct, perhaps blunt question, Jennah?"

He saw the moment her guard slipped into place.

"If I may reserve the right to not answer."

"Of course. I'm here to help, not hurt or diminish what progress you may have achieved to date."

She acknowledged his comment with a slight nod.

Jeremy put down his pen, clasped his hands on the desk and gazed directly into her eyes. "How badly do you want to be helped? Or do you truly, deep down desire that at all?"

Reactions raced over her features like dark thunder clouds rolled across an already sullen sky...shock, anger, self-pity. Then came the tears. One lonely drop followed by a slow but steady trickle.

"You think I'm so pathetic I'd do all this just for attention?"

Jeremy shook his head. "No, I don't."

"Then why would you ask me such a thing?"

He rose from his chair and walked around to lean against the front of his desk, arms folded in a seemingly relaxed manner across his midsection. Yet, from his constant study of the body and its intricate systems, he knew the position shielded his energetic body from absorbing the negative vibes bouncing off his patient.

"Admitting you need help is only one part of being healed. You have to believe in yourself and your ability to get past the emotions that've held you captive, and trust that wholeness waits on the other side of treatment. Otherwise, it's all a waste of precious time and energy."

"Well, it's my time and energy!"

He sighed. "And mine."

"But I'm *paying* for yours."

"Then it's also a waste of money if you don't truly desire to be healed. Let me ask, Jennah, do you know the definition of insanity?"

Her back went ramrod straight against the chair. "What are you insinuating now?"

"Not a thing, just asking a simple question."

"I don't know... severe craziness or something to that effect. I have no idea the technical definition, but I can only imagine what that might be."

Jeremy smiled. "I'm not talking about the medical or technical definition. Albert Einstein said the definition of insanity is 'doing the same thing over and over, expecting a different outcome.' If you're not willing to take a few risks and perhaps do something you haven't done before, then meeting with me will not accomplish the results you're capable of achieving."

He gave her a few moments to digest that information before asking, "Are you willing to at least consider alternative therapies?"

After several minutes of silence so tense it screamed obscenities at him, he sensed her relent a tad. She took a deep breath and blew her nose into the wad of tissue he handed her then raised tear-drenched eyes to his. "I'm willing to try. As long as I can do it alone."

Jeremy offered her a hand and helped her rise from her seat. "Agreed. For now."

Doubt and fear clouded her expression.

He cocooned both of her hands in his. "Trust me, Jennah. I'm not just another psychotherapist. I am also a life coach, spiritual mentor, and energy medicine practitioner. I've been doing this a long time—I've dealt with folks exhibiting illnesses and phobias much worse than I believe yours to be. We'll take things one step at a time and when you're ready, we'll consider other options besides one-on-one sessions. Together, we can get you to a place of wholeness."

"I pray you're right, Dr. Hinton, because honestly, you're my last hope. I don't know how much more of this I can take."

He walked with her to the lobby. "Angela will give you a journal. For the next two weeks, I'd like for you to record your thoughts, feelings, fears, hopes, dreams...anything and everything you'd like to see changed in your life. Make a point to list one or two things you're grateful for each day also.

"Express these in words or drawings, however you feel most comfortable and free. Bring it with you to your next appointment and we'll figure out what to do next."

He waited while Angela handed Jennah the book and a pack of colored pens and scheduled her next appointment, and then escorted her to the door with a few more words of encouragement and instruction.

"Whew!" He leaned against the door totally drained. "When is my next arrival?"

Angela glanced at the schedule on her desk. "A half hour from now."

"Wonderful. I'll be back by then."

Jeremy left the office, as he often did, to stroll the sidewalks of Middletown, Connecticut. Annabelle smooth leaf hydrangea shrubs bloomed between strategically placed native evergreens. Their scent mingled with the patches of wild red columbine, bearberry and wild ginger also planted between the sidewalk and street.

As always, the beauty of nature restored his mental and emotional balance, which is why he had Angela schedule enough time between appointments to indulge in a foray several times a day. Weather permitting of course. Twenty minutes later, he returned to his office refreshed and ready to take on his next client.

Chapter Five

Keri left her office, her emotions on overload. Her entire day had consisted of dealing with one irate client after another. She'd missed lunch and both breaks. Her attempts to keep God uppermost in her thoughts had been useless. Now all she wanted to do was get home, close the curtains, and curl up in her chair—after a long, hot bubble bath.

Before she crossed the threshold into her apartment, her cell phone rang.

"Hello?"

"Hey, sweetheart, how was your day?"

"Awful." She couldn't even face a chat with Jeremy at the moment. "Can I call you back in a while?"

"Sure."

She breathed her thanks, thumbed the 'off' button and restrained herself from tossing the phone across the room. A quick detour through the kitchen to grab a bottle of water, then she escaped into the bathroom. After a half hour steeped in frothy water, surrounded by scented candles and soft music, she felt more like herself.

In her favorite pajamas, with dinner over and the kitchen back in order, she retired to the living room, sank into what she now deemed her meditation chair and returned Jeremy's call.

"Hey there."

"Hi! You OK?"

"Yeah, just a rough day dealing with whiny, rude people."

"Boy, do I know what you mean. Dealt with a couple of those myself today."

They exchanged pleasantries and told each other about their respective day, then Keri hung up, determined to spend quality time with God before crashing for the night.

Hours later she drifted up from a deep sleep to the whisper of her name.

"What?" she mumbled, not quite awake enough to be afraid.

"Wake up, Keri," the voice lured.

She rolled over, swiped a hand across her mouth and tried to focus but couldn't seem to pull herself out of sleep mode.

"Sorry," she whispered, and dozed off once more.

When her alarm went off at five thirty, she dragged herself from beneath the covers and into the shower. Only after her first cup of coffee did she recall the voice in the night.

"Was that You, God?" she wondered aloud. "Did I miss a divine appointment or something?"

The question haunted her throughout the day. When Jeremy called that evening, she told him what had happened, anxious to hear his opinion on what the voice in her dreams may have meant.

"Has that ever happened to you?" she asked.

"Sometimes," Jeremy answered. "I've also heard that when you have trouble sleeping it's because you're awake in someone else's dream."

She laughed. "Were you dreaming about me then?"

He chuckled. "Always."

"Well, please don't tonight. I need a good night's rest."

They laughed together, and then he sobered. "Seriously, though, I've often heard God wakes people in the middle of the night, or early morning hours because that's when they're more susceptible to suggestion and most likely to actually hear and pay attention to what He has to say. Try to wake up if it happens again. Many spiritual leaders say they get their best sermons or writing done between three and four a.m. Have you not heard what Rumi said about morning breezes?"

"Not that I can recall."

"The morning breezes have secrets to tell, don't go back to sleep," Jeremy quoted. "Rumi believed people were missing out on what God had to say to them about the questions in their lives because when they awoke in the middle of the night, instead of praying and seeking answers, they forced themselves to roll over and go back to sleep.

"Remember also, God woke Samuel in the middle of the night three times before Eli realized what was happening and told him when God called his name again, to respond with 'Speak, Lord for your servant is listening.'"

"Well, I tried to wake up but just couldn't seem to open my eyes or clear my mind. I'll try harder next time."

"Good and keep your journal beside the bed just in case you want to jot down the inspiration or insight you receive. Don't be upset if it doesn't happen again right away. Sometimes God works gently to get our attention before He establishes a set time to meet with us. And sometimes He may do this for a particular reason or until the message He is trying to get to you comes across, then the meetings will end.

"I've heard preachers and authors, even artists, say God woke them at a certain time every morning until their project was done, but not after." Jeremy seemed determined to help her understand.

"The truth is, God is always speaking to us. We've just got to get into the habit of listening with our whole heart and mind and being open to hear when He does. You've been practicing this more lately than ever before in your life. Could be that since you had such a rough day yesterday, God wanted to give you comfort or perhaps wisdom or instruction about a certain client or something. Happens to me all the time."

When she prepared for bed that evening, Keri made sure to place her journal on the nightstand. She crawled beneath the covers and prayed. "Lord, if You desire to speak to me tonight, please help me to awaken fully so I can hear You."

She tumbled into a deep, dreamless sleep and awoke the next morning to sunlight streaming into her windows and the alarm clock blaring. Realizing she'd overslept, she hurried through her morning routine but had to relegate her prayer time to during her commute to work.

That evening, after working overtime, she dragged herself home and collapsed into bed without a single thought of hearing God's voice or meeting with Him anytime during the night.

Chapter Six

Keri woke Saturday morning too tired to motivate herself out of bed. She lay for a long time, even dozed somewhat until her bladder forced her to rise. After a quick trip to the bathroom, she stumbled into the kitchen.

"I'm so tired today, Lord." She yawned and stretched while her morning coffee brewed.

After retrieving and answering three text messages on her cell phone, she listened to voicemail, but didn't return those calls. She'd do that after some quiet time with God.

Cup of coffee in hand, she sank into the leather chair matching the loveseat in her living room. Her gaze roamed the cozy space, thankful for her lovely apartment and the job she loved which allowed her to afford it.

The small apartment complex had been constructed on a piece of property just outside

Middletown city limits and consisted of six units containing four apartments each. The complex was surrounded by a small forest through which a tiny creek tumbled across moss-covered rocks. Each building boasted ancient architecture of wood and stone, and the apartments—small and cozy—blended right in with the rural setting. Rich wood, antique fixtures and soft colors made the one-bedroom efficiency seem like a lone cottage tucked away in the thickets.

Unlike most modern multiplexes, these units were so well insulated one barely heard the neighbors. Every home included a private balcony and a small terrace that opened out onto a spacious field that flowed into the wooded area.

No tennis courts, swimming pools or fitness centers, only a field of wildflowers, a natural walking path and plenty of trees and underbrush to spark the imagination of children who resided within the compound.

As her mind continued to wander, Keri relaxed into a blessed serenity she'd sought but hadn't quite felt all week. She'd always heard the rhetoric of a full moon bringing out the crazy in folks but had never experienced it to the degree she'd seen this past week.

Arguments among clients and staff at the accounting firm where she worked had everyone on edge so much that her normal lunch routine was often late, short, or skipped altogether. She felt it too, on every level. Mental exhaustion, physical fatigue and emotional lethargy clouded her entire being so that all she desired was to stay inside, pajama-clad, and do as little as possible today.

The grandfather clock chimed. Once owned by her mom's great grandparents, the old timepiece reminded Keri of everything she'd committed to this day.

As she uncurled her legs and stood, a wave of dizziness swept over her.

"Whoa." She sank back into the chair, her heart pounding hard. A cold sweat slithered along her flesh. She took several deep breaths and waited for the moment of weakness to pass.

"OK, Lord, I don't know what's going on here. I'm hardly ever sick, and one week of madness shouldn't result in my feeling so terrible. Help me make it through this day."

When she felt strong enough, she walked a bit unsteadily into the bathroom and indulged in a long, hot shower. She'd barely finished dressing and drying her hair when a knock sounded on her front door.

She swung the door open and smiled at Jeremy. A frown creased his brow as he stepped inside.

"What's wrong, Keri? You don't look so well."

She shrugged and led the way into the kitchen. "Just not feeling a hundred percent today."

"Why didn't you call? I'm sure your parents wouldn't want you out if you're not feeling well."

"It'll pass. Just been a stressful week, threw my normal routine into a tailspin. I'm probably still reeling from it. My parents have been waiting to meet you since the moment I mentioned your name to mom."

He laughed. "Yeah, my mom is anxious to meet you too. Seems no matter how old we get, we're still their babies."

Keri agreed and grabbed her purse from the counter. A wave of nausea slammed her, and she clutched the counter.

Jeremy rushed to catch her as her knees gave way. "OK, enough. You're not going anywhere. C'mon, let's get you off your feet."

He carried her into the living room and stretched her out as much as possible on the loveseat. Grabbing an afghan off the back of her chair, he covered her as shivers trembled through her body.

"Sorry." Keri muttered an apology, embarrassed despite how sick she felt.

He brushed a hand across her brow. "Hey, no need to apologize. I'll call your mom. Where's your phone?"

Keri pulled it out her back pocket.

"Great. What can I get you? You don't feel feverish. Yet. So, how about a glass of water or cup of tea?"

Keri shook her head, rolled over and drifted off.

* * * * *

Stunned and worried, Jeremy scrolled through her recent call list until he found the one marked 'mom' and hit the send button. His heart stumbled a bit when Keri's mother answered.

"Hi, honey! On your way yet?"

The woman sounded just like Keri over the phone. Jeremy cleared his throat. "Um, hello Mrs. Jackson. It's Jeremy. I'm afraid Keri's not feeling well. I arrived this morning to pick her up for our lunch date with you and Mr. Jackson and found her pale and shaking. She almost fainted."

"Oh, my. I'll be right over." Mrs. Jackson hung up before Jeremy could say another word.

He brushed the hair off Keri's cheeks. She was sticky with sweat and shaking. He went into the bathroom and wet a washcloth with cool water, then pulled the spread off of her bed and carried both back into the living room. He placed the cloth on her head then folded the spread a couple of times over and added it to the afghan which already covered her.

Stroking the damp rag over her forehead and face with one hand, he closed his eyes and envisioned her surrounded by light. He prayed while scanning her body for energy imbalances with his free hand.

"God, let Your healing energy and the blood of Jesus cleanse and protect Keri from whatever is trying to attack her body. Archangel Raphael, by the power of Christ, heal Keri."

Before he could determine which, if any incongruities were present in her energy system, a knock sounded on the door. He rose and opened it to the woman who, without a doubt, gave birth to Keri. She bustled through the entrance, asking questions in such rapid succession, he didn't have a chance to answer.

Keri stirred when her mother knelt beside her and called her name.

"Hey, mom," she mumbled.

"What's going on, Keri?"

She shook her head slightly. "Don't know. Just tired and a headache."

"Let's get you propped up a bit." Mrs. Jackson slid her arms beneath her daughter to help, then turned to Jeremy. "I'm Mattie, by the way. Would you see if she has some pain reliever or fever reducing medicine somewhere? Where would it be, sweetheart?"

"Bedside...table...drawer," Keri rasped. "I don't feel good. Mom..." Her words trailed off as Keri slid back into a semi-sleep state.

"I think we should get her to a hospital." Jeremy hated seeing her so weak and sick.

Mattie shook her head. "Probably too soon for that. In all of my years dealing with Keri's childhood ailments, I've learned that most doctors prefer symptoms to be present forty-eight hours or so before making an emergency room visit—unless things get really bad, of course. We'll just watch her for a bit. Go ahead and get that OTC medicine and we'll keep it handy for when she rouses again."

Jeremy did as she asked and then pulled the ottoman over so Mattie could sit by her daughter. He settled himself in the opulent leather chair next to the love seat where Keri lay.

Within a couple of hours, Keri's condition worsened. Jeremy's heart raced as she convulsed in her mother's arms while they waited for an ambulance. When the paramedics arrived, he did his best to answer their questions, then followed when they rushed her to the nearest emergency room. Her mother called Keri's father, then talked with the triage nurse. Jeremy called his mom, who promised to be there soon and join them in the wait.

Sunni arrived in her usual flourish—dressed in the hippie fashion of the sixties, adorned in braids and beads, crosses and feathers. But Jeremy had never been happier to see her. He realized, not for the first time, he had her to thank for his chosen career. Her deep spirituality had enabled him to grow up with an open heart and mind which, in turn, sparked his intrigue with all things homeopathic. He made introductions to Keri's parents and the four chatted amicably, careful to keep a positive outlook despite the lack of information on Keri's condition.

Thirty minutes later, any optimism they felt dimmed when the ER doctor called them into a private room.

"Well, we're not sure what's going on. Looks to be some form of infection but until blood tests come back we won't be positive whether viral or bacterial. Has she been out of the country or exposed to anyone who's been overseas lately?"

Stunned, everyone looked at each other, and then shrugged.

"She works in an accounting office. We've no idea who she may have been in contact with," Jeremy said.

The doctor's sigh spoke volumes. "Well, all we can do at the moment is wait and watch. We won't even know what we're treating until we get the blood work back and run more tests."

"Can we see her?" Mattie asked.

"I'd advise minimal contact until we know what we're dealing with and whether it is contagious. I'll keep you all posted as we know more."

Moments after the doctor left, a hospital volunteer came in with coffee, tea, water and a tray of snacks. Jeremy and Keri's father, Doug, took turns pacing the tiny room while the women joined hands in prayer. An hour after he'd left, the doctor returned.

"We've found a rare strain of bacteria in Keri's bloodstream and have her on very strong antibiotics. She's slipped into an unconscious state, but that's common with this type of situation. Since we don't know a whole lot about this particular virus, and we're not sure how or from whom she contracted it, we'd like to check anyone who intends to visit with her to make sure you're not a carrier."

"But we have never been overseas." Mattie's protest was seconded by Doug.

"It's been years and years for me, and I've never met Keri," Sunni said. "And Jeremy's never been overseas."

"I understand. But since it is so rare and we have very little to go on, I'd rather be safe than sorry. We'll also monitor each of you to make sure you don't become infected."

All four agreed to the blood tests. They waited while a phlebotomist was summoned, and then waited for the results.

"All this darn waiting," Doug grumbled.

Everyone murmured in agreement.

Two hours later, the doctor returned to assure each of them they were free of any bacterial and viral possibilities, and that the staff had moved Keri into a stepdown unit adjacent to ICU. Since no more than two people were allowed in to see her at once, Doug and Mattie went first. Ten minutes later, Doug appeared, pale and shaken, and sent Jeremy in.

"Mattie doesn't want to leave her."

"That's understandable," Sunni said. "But she'll need to rest and take care of herself. I know we've just met, but I can assure you, Jeremy is very fond of your daughter. We'd be honored to take our turns in keeping vigil with you and Mattie."

"Thanks, we appreciate that. I'm sure Mattie will call her sister and niece also. My brother, his wife and their son may want to take turns too. If this doesn't turn around quickly I'm sure we'll be making phone calls." He clenched a fist, slammed it into his other palm. "Just wish we knew what to expect."

They turned when Mattie walked in the room. "Jeremy is beside himself. I'll give you a moment with him," she told Sunni.

Sunni thanked her and went in to check on her son. He gazed up at her from the chair by Keri's bed, his eyes revealing his devastation.

"Mom, she's the only woman I've ever felt this strongly about. What am I going to do now?"

She put her arms around him, hugged hard, then cupped his face in her hands. "You're going to put everything you've learned into practice. We'll create an environment of wellness around her so strong, she'll have no choice but to return to us healed, whole and complete."

Chapter Seven

She awoke in another dimension. Keri had no idea if she was in Heaven, but neither did she fear Hell. Her surroundings were reminiscent of a dense forest at dusk. Shadows danced against a sunset where brilliant colors bled from the sky. A light shone in the distance but as she moved toward it, Keri felt as though she plowed through molasses. Unease pricked her skin. The sound of water drew her deeper into the woods until she stood at the base of a vast waterfall and rapids so swift she dared not attempt to cross the river.

The light grew stronger, brighter. Beckoning.

I need to get to the light.

The moment the thought reverberated through her a bridge appeared over the fast-moving current. A rainbow arched the sky above it. Prisms of color swirled at her feet as she stepped onto the sturdy wooden structure. The farther she traversed, the brighter the hues until it seemed her entire being absorbed the spiraling tones of pure energy. Every detail of her surroundings magnified until she became part of the lush, pulsating environment.

As she stepped onto the thick, satiny grass on the other side of the river, the bridge dissipated behind her. Keri shivered and her heartbeat quickened in cadence to the throb of a drum far off in the distance. She breathed in the heavenly scent of wildflowers that grew throughout the large, lovely meadow. Before her, behind her, to the left and to the right, plants displayed beautiful blooms of every size, shape, color, and texture imaginable.

A deep, robin's egg-blue sky vibrated with light and color. The deeper she moved into the field, the closer she came to what she now recognized as a city, located on a hill at the far end of the pasture.

As she approached a fence which surrounded the municipality, she recognized things she'd read about in the Bible. Gates of pearl, a huge wall inset with gemstones of every kind.... ruby, sapphire, and emerald.

Keri stood transfixed as the sound of chimes and a chant of "holy, holy, holy," filled the air.

"I'm in Heaven," she breathed and for a moment sadness filled her heart. Before she could process the emotions welling within her breast, the opulent gate opened and Spark and her sister appeared, only this time the child was older.

"Hi, Keri!"

As it had in her previous vision, the little girl's voice radiated joy.

"I died?"

The girl shook her head. "Your body is under attack, but you're safe here with us. God says you'll go back soon. While you wait, there are some people here who want to meet and greet you."

A young man approached. He appeared to be about thirty years old, and Keri gasped as she recognized Jeremy in the face of the stranger. Then she remembered he'd told her his father died when he was a toddler.

The man embraced her, and Keri felt a love so great she thought she'd burst with it. Ancestors she'd never met but somehow recognized poured out into the field until she was surrounded by people who loved her.

* * * * *

Keri walked with her sister along the banks of a meadow brook, amazed at how they communicated without opening their mouths.

Water trickled over rocks in a melody that reminded her of the wind chimes she'd heard at home. Every tree and flower glowed with life, their colors deep and vibrant. The thing that fascinated her most was how every thought manifested into living form almost before she completed it.

She wished to see butterflies, and they swarmed about her. A bumblebee droned in ecstasy over a daisy as he tasted the sweet nectar of the bright yellow center. The happy faces of pansies smiled up from where they bloomed at her feet. Rose buds opened as she passed the bush, their scent perfuming the air with fragrance so rich, it defied explanation.

"How long will I be here?"

"There is no time in eternity. You'll be here as long as God deems necessary."

"Well, if I'm going to be with you a while, what shall I call you?"

The girl laughed and the sound of her joy filled Keri with an inexpressible delight. "Just call me Blossom."

"That fits," Keri said. "Will I see Jesus and the Father?"

Before Blossom could respond, Jesus stood before them. Keri gasped in awe at His radiant splendor. She knelt. "My Lord."

He lifted her from her knees and into His embrace. Warmth and love flooded her being. Was it possible to burst with emotion? Her questions about His birth sprang forth. Jesus smiled and her tension eased.

"Patience, my child. All will be answered in due season."

Chapter Eight

Jeremy pulled into his spot in the parking garage a few minutes shy of midnight. He'd always loved coming home to the lush beauty of his townhouse, but never to this degree. The last thirty-six plus hours had been torture.

Keri's condition fluctuated so much they didn't know what to expect from one moment to the next. The doctors monitored her at regular intervals. Since she'd been admitted yesterday morning, a constant batter of blood work, ultrasounds, and other tests had been performed. They'd inserted a shunt to help drain excess fluids from her brain.

He, his mother, and Keri's parents had gotten to know each other pretty well over the last day and a half. Jeremy looked forward to spending more time with them, despite the circumstances.

But tonight, he needed quality prayer and meditation time and a few hours of sleep before his workday began in the morning. He unlocked the door, opened it, and stepped through. In an instant, tension eased from his shoulders.

First order of things was a shower and shave. As he went about those tasks, he tried to empty his mind of worldly distractions. If he could and focus on the Holy Spirit, wisdom and intuition would replace worry and upset. But his efforts went unrewarded, as his thoughts continued to circle around Keri's condition.

When the water ran tepid, Jeremy turned it off, toweled dry and slipped into his pajamas. Out of habit, he wiped down the bath and carried his dirty laundry downstairs to the utility room. He stopped in the kitchen for a drink of water, and then headed up the stairs, bypassing the chair where he sometimes meditated.

Crossing the threshold of the spare bedroom which served as his prayer room, Jeremy took a deep, cleansing breath and gazed around with gratitude for the blessing of his home.

The first time he viewed the old Brownstone five years ago, he'd known this place was for him. Though the architect had updated the place, he'd maintained the integrity of the home and the time period in which it was constructed. Rich wood, antique fixtures, and soft carpeting wove together to create an atmosphere of sheer tranquility.

Foregoing his customary journaling routine, Jeremy crossed to the tiny altar, lit candles, and then knelt on a huge pillow which lay on the special rug he'd purchased because its tapestry design—a work of art in itself—made him think of peaceful sunsets over a deserted beach.

Arms open wide in supplication, he prayed. "Dear God, open my eyes that I may see, my ears that I may hear and my heart that I may understand what is happening. Keri is everything I've ever dreamed of in a woman—all I want in a wife. She's beautiful and talented, gifted and funny, and hungers for a deep relationship with You."

Tears clogged his throat, welled in his eyes. He fought them a moment and then let go of the struggle. "I can't do this on my own. My mind and emotions are in turmoil. I trust You, God, and I entrust Keri into Your loving embrace. Please show me what, if anything, I am supposed to do to help her."

He waited, determined not to move until he had wisdom and clear direction. When doubt and fear filled his mind with incessant chatter, he repeated the words, "Be still and know God," until peace reigned in his thoughts once more.

Jeremy meditated on the goodness of God and all he'd known and learned over the years of his childhood and subsequent spiritual growth as an adult. At last, words settled in his spirit: "Teach and practice what you know."

Visions of what he understood and believed about the body's ability to heal itself flashed through his brain like a movie reel, until blessed assurance put his spirit to rest. He retired to his chair, picked up his "Keri journal" and recorded his thoughts, feelings, concerns and impressions until clarity shone through. Now he knew, without a doubt, what to do.

Jeremy awoke the next morning positive Keri would get through this experience and return to him as his mother predicted—healed, whole and complete. After his last client left for the day, he told Angela to text him should the need arise, and then went to the hospital where he found Mattie and Doug in the ICU waiting room.

"Any change?"

Mattie shook her head. "More tests." That explained why they weren't in Keri's room. "You just missed your mom."

Before he could respond, the doctor strode into the room to report his findings from the latest tests. He also told them Keri was back in her room.

Jeremy cleared his throat. "Before you go, I'd really like to speak to you and Mr. and Mrs. Jackson about some things."

The doctor nodded and gave them his full attention.

"I know it may sound a little alternative, but I'd like to use essential oils and do a lymphatic massage on Keri."

The doctor eyed him a moment. "What kind of oils?"

"Well, oregano has antibacterial properties. Turmeric and ginger are anti-inflammatories. Peppermint cleanses the lymphatic system;

juniper helps the body throw off toxic wastes and lavender is calming."

"Sounds like you know what you're doing."

"Yes, sir, I've studied and practiced holistic healing for years and have found essential oils beneficial for myself and many of my patients."

"You're a doctor?"

"Psychotherapist."

"I see. And how will you apply them?"

"Some, like lavender, are safe to use directly on her wrists or massaged into the bottom of her feet. The stronger ones are mixed with a 'carrier' such as extra virgin olive oil. I'd also like to place a blend of them in a reed diffuser to help purify the air."

"We have to be careful of electronics and even battery operated items because of interference with these machines."

"A reed diffuser uses no electronics. It's a bottle filled with the reeds, or sticks, which soak up the oils and release them into the air."

The doctor hesitated as though considering, then rolled his head and shoulders with a heavy sigh. "I'll give the go-ahead for this but be very careful. Use gloves at all times. If I see any adverse change in Keri's condition, I'll put a halt to it at once. Oh, and make sure those compression socks are always back on her feet once you're done."

"Thank you," Jeremy said, and then turned to Mattie and Doug when the doctor left the room. "Is this OK with the two of you?"

Mattie smiled and touched his arm. "You do what you feel led to do. We're going to keep the prayer chains going."

Jeremy grinned. "I know it might seem strange and weird, but trust me, Mattie, I will be using prayer and meditation also. God created us as both physical and spiritual beings."

* * * * *

Jeremy arrived at the hospital after work as he'd done for the past three days to relieve Mattie for a few hours. "How is she?"

Mattie shook her head. "Not much different from what I can tell, and no one has told me otherwise. I drifted off today and dreamed I was with her."

Jeremy smiled. "The bond between mother and child is never broken, so on some level you probably were.

Tears welled in her eyes. "I hope so. I keep talking to her, telling her how much we love her and that we're praying for her and all that, but I still feel helpless."

Jeremy put his arm around her shoulder. "I know. So do I sometimes, but I believe without a shadow of a doubt that she'll pull through this. We all will. And who knows what good will come from this experience?"

Mattie sighed. "I sure hope so."

"Go home and get some rest, Mattie. You've got to take care of yourself. She may need you to aide in her recovery."

Mattie leaned over and kissed her daughter on the forehead, whispered something in her ear and then left.

Instead of settling in the chair, Jeremy stood at the bedside and prayed for the Holy Spirit to surround Keri as the blood of Jesus cleansed, healed, renewed, and restored her own blood to perfection. The evening shift nurse assigned to her care came in to check vital signs.

"What are these bottles, oils, and things for?" she asked, her wave encompassing the religious figurines, vials of holy water and oil, as well as the diffuser and essential oils Jeremy had brought.

"All tools for spiritual and holistic healing."

She rolled her eyes, and snorted, her mouth drawn into a frown. "You people need to realize she may not come out of this and if she does, she may never be the same. There's no telling how this infection will affect her brain and body. She could very well be in a vegetative state the rest of her natural life."

Jeremy bit back the many retorts that sprang to mind but before he could form a response, his mother walked into the room.

"And you people need to realize there is more to a person than a brain and body. We are spiritual beings having an earthly experience. Keri's body can and will respond to the strength and faith of our thoughts and prayers. We understand your position from your years of education, training, and experience, but if you can't accept our views, or at the very least, support our efforts, we'll ask that you be removed from her care."

The nurse mumbled an apology and fled.

"Thank you, Mom." Jeremy swallowed the knot of emotion clogging his airways as his mother enfolded him in her embrace.

"How are you holding up my love?"

"Better, now that you're here."

Sunni smiled and stroked the hair off his forehead, a familiar gesture from as far back as he could remember.

"Put all negativity out of your mind." She rubbed a thumb across the worry line between his eyes.

"I am, Mom, but what if it's God's will that Keri not recover? I'm afraid, more than I've ever been about anything. Ever."

"I know and understand. Nowhere is it written we can't feel or express fear. It's what we do with those emotions that count. Now I think you need to get out of here early and go home. Pray, meditate and get some rest."

"But I just got here."

"OK, stay awhile, then, but make it a short

while this time."

Jeremy grinned. "Yes, ma'am."

After a few moments of discussion, he and Sunni held hands over Keri and prayed for the healing power of God to do its perfect work in her.

An hour later he followed his mother's advice and went home, where he spent yet another hour in prayer and meditation only to rise the next morning and begin the routine all over again.

* * * * *

Jeremy pulled into his parking spot and groaned. His first patient of the day was Jennah Anderson. He glanced around, relieved to see only Angela's car in the small lot in front of his office.

The moment he stepped through the entrance, his eyes fell on a beautiful arrangement of fruit, cut to look like flowers. He glanced at Angela, his eyebrow arched in question.

"From your first client." She smiled and handed him the card.

I am grateful for you....

"Well, how's that for an early morning boost?" He grinned. "Ring me when she arrives, will you?"

Angela nodded and handed him his messages.

In his office, he closed the door and eased into the chair. He flipped through the slips of paper and decided nothing couldn't wait until after his first appointment. Resting his head against the soft, buttery leather, he took several, deep breaths. Every time his mind circled back to Keri's condition, he reined it in to focus on relaxation and preparation for the meeting about to occur. By the time Angela buzzed to announce Jennah's arrival, he was ready.

He walked around his desk to greet her just as she opened the door and stepped into the room. "Good morning. Thank you for the lovely fruit arrangement. I take it you've had a good week?"

Her entire face lit up when Jennah smiled. "Actually, I have. I've never felt so hopeful in my entire life." She handed him the journal he'd given her on her last visit.

"Recording things on these pages has really opened my eyes to the negative thoughts that control my mind."

"Really? That's wonderful. Most people take a few weeks or months before they realize that."

She laughed. "To be honest, the first couple of days were tough. Those questions you asked really dug deep. Stung in ways I'd never experienced or expected. So, when you thumb through that, you'll see some pretty scathing comments. But then it's like a vein opened and a lot of those old feelings poured out, and then just disappeared.

"I never realized all the things—people, places, experiences—I have to be grateful for until I started listing them. I decided to not only recognize but acknowledge and act on that gratitude—hence the fruit. It's like a whole new world has opened up for me."

Jeremy gestured for her to sit, then resumed his seat behind the desk. "I'd hoped that would happen. Tell me, Jennah, do you like to read?"

"I love to read!"

"Would you be interested in reading books that explain what's happened to you and how you can continue healing your life by reprogramming your mind?"

She nodded.

Jeremy opened the drawer where he kept a healthy supply of literature on the power of positive thought, prayer, and speech and handed her a few volumes.

"Start with these. If you enjoy them, more resources are listed in each book. Feel free to peruse those while I skim through this." He picked up her journal.

True to her word, the first several pages were filled with doubts and fears, hope followed by curses and expletives. She didn't even begin her gratitude list for a few days, but once she did, things turned around rather quickly. They chatted a little longer while he made notes in her chart. When their time together drew to a close, Jeremy assured her she'd made great strides, but warned that complete change could take some time.

"So, if you wake up one day all gloomy and depressed, don't be surprised. When we start a path of self-awareness and healing, old habits tend to rear up and try to regain the ground they've lost. Are you a praying woman, Jennah?"

"I'm a Christian."

"Good. Study Romans 12:2, where Paul exhorts us to renew our minds. Remember, when the devil attacks you with negative thoughts, don't dwell on them. Just let them flow through—like the proverbial 'in one ear and out the other.'

"In other words, if you find yourself ruminating about your body in a way that is *not* how you'd like to think and feel, simply speak aloud, something to the effect of, "That's how I used to feel, but the truth is..." And replace the negative thought with something positive.

"Also, if you get really anxious or upset, take deep breaths. It only takes between sixteen and eighteen seconds to interrupt your current thought pattern. So, take deep breaths while speaking the positive statement or statements. We're on the right path, Jennah. I'm excited for you and can't wait to see how the next two weeks unfold."

Jeremy rose and escorted her into the lobby. "Angela will make your next appointment. But if you find yourself in a bind between now and then, please don't hesitate to come in before your scheduled time."

She thanked him and left.

Jeremy took his usual brisk walk between clients and then returned to resume the process for the remainder of his workday. After his last patient, he decided to take another stroll instead of rushing to the hospital. He breathed in the heavenly scent of earth and flowers along his usual path while he prayed.

"God, You are all knowing, omnipotent and omnipresent, and I trust You with Keri's wellbeing. But my faith is wavering and, although I try not to be, I am weary and afraid. If I may be so bold as to ask... please, Lord, give me a sign that You really are with Keri, and she'll be OK whatever the outcome of this battle."

He stumbled, nearly fell, then bent down to see what he'd tripped over. Jeremy eyed the raw beauty of a rock unlike any he'd ever seen but had somehow managed to kick up. The moment he touched the stone, an image flashed in his mind and gelled—a custom gold mounting attached to a sturdy chain. Keri could wear the stone nestled against her heart.

Jeremy headed straight to the jewelry shop three blocks from his office. Trovosky Jewelers had been in business for nearly a hundred years. Each son or daughter who inherited the shop had done his or her best to bring the establishment into the current decade while maintaining its old world charm and the ingrained ethics that had also passed from generation to generation.

He'd wandered in on occasion while on his

daily walk, always amazed when he left, inevitably with a gift for his mother or some other special lady in his life, whether a romantic interest or a friend.

"Jeremy, my boy! How are you?" Mr. Trovosky greeted him as he entered the store.

"I'm good. How's your family?"

"Everyone's fine. How's that young lady of yours? Any change?"

Jeremy smiled. "Not a whole lot of change either way, but we're still hopeful. Which is why I'm here. I'd like to have this mounted and hung on the best chain you have."

He handed the stone to the senior Trovosky, who instantly produced a jeweler's loupe and began examining it. His eyes lit with awe when he gazed at Jeremy again. "This is pure peridot, rare and precious. Where did you get it?"

"Actually, I practically tripped over this on the sidewalk a few minutes ago. Since I'd been in prayer and asking God for a sign, I took it as one and thought I'd have it made into a necklace for Keri."

The gentleman nodded. "I have just the setting. Won't take long."

With that, he disappeared into the back room. Jeremy checked his phone to see if there were any messages from his mother or either of the Jacksons. Relieved there wasn't, he slid it into his trouser pocket. His fingers drummed on the counter as he waited. Ten minutes. Twenty. Before the clock behind the counter hand moved to thirty, Mr. Trovosky walked through the curtain separating his workshop from the retail area.

"Here you go." He swung the necklace into Jeremy's palm.

The stone nestled inside an intricate gold setting and hung from a hardy rope chain. Jeremy stared at his find, which had become a work of art. "This is beautiful. Perfect."

"I've had that old mounting for nearly as long as I've been alive, with no idea what I'd do with it, much less why I hung on to it. The moment you laid that peridot crystal in my hand, I knew this is exactly what it's been waiting for."

The jeweler turned the nugget where it caught and reflected the overhead glow. "Such a precious gem needs to be cradled, not wrapped in wire. This particular encasement will allow light refraction from any angle."

The piece seemed to pulsate in Jeremy's hand. He tugged his wallet out of his back pocket and handed the jeweler his credit card.

Trovosky slid the receipt across the counter. "Would you like me to box that up for you?"

"No thanks." Jeremy slipped the necklace into his shirt pocket. "I'll just keep it close to my heart."

Chapter Nine

Keri basked in the warm glow of light that always shone in the heavenly realm. Its exquisite beauty would forever be etched in her mind and heart. She relished this time and experience with her sister, but the physical world pulled at her. Today she and Blossom would embark on a journey into the truth—as her sister had termed the excursion.

"I don't understand. How can one journey *into* truth?"

Blossom's smile reflected that of every other living creature in this place. "Understanding will come, Keri. You'll see. Everything you think, speak, or do has the potential to enrich your life. Come, now, let's be on our way."

With that indictment, Blossom mounted Spark and urged Keri up behind her. Spark eased into a smooth, steady gait. Awe and wonder sizzled through Keri and filled her with an inexplicable joy.

"Pay attention."

The words, softly spoken in a voice different from her sister's, swirled then calmed Keri's emotions, and she took in the scenery.

"Do you see?"

Again, the voice resounded through her.

"What am I looking for?"

"Truth. Look closely and truth will appear."

Then she saw. What she witnessed hit her with a force so great she nearly tumbled from the horse's back.

Far away lay an open field just outside a small village. Crisp and cool, the air zinged through her. As they drew near, she knew what lay before them.

A manger.

A young woman held a tiny babe to her breast as men and animals bowed.

Jesus.

The beloved name whispered through her entire being. Keri gazed in astonishment. Though the air smarted and a small fire burned, the temperature felt more like fall than winter.

"So, He was born in the fall?" Keri asked Blossom.

Before her sister could answer, Spark picked up speed and continued. As he galloped on, Keri's face stung from ice in the air. The scene appeared before her again—a manger in an open field just outside a settlement. Snow covered the ground and thatched roof of the stable where the young woman held her babe, wrapped in warm swaddling.

"It's winter for sure, but..."

"Don't think, Keri, listen with your heart, understand with your spirit."

Again, the voice was unlike Blossom's. Spark ascended into motion, and as they continued on, Keri began to realize that, although the exhibition remained basically the same.... a structure in a field outside of a township or encampment. They traveled through each of the four seasons common to the earthly sphere and then *truth* embedded itself into the very fiber of her being.

Even as she realized the significance of what she'd perceived, Spark veered off the path into the woods. He halted near the waterfall and rapids she'd crossed when she'd entered this magnificent kingdom.

Keri hugged Blossom close. "I'm leaving now, aren't I?"

"Soon."

"Will I ever see you again?"

Blossom climbed off Spark's back and waited for her to do the same. "I'm always with you, Keri. Remember that. Tell mom and dad too."

"I promise. I'll never forget this time with you. Will you come to me again as you did before, in a vision or dream?"

Blossom's smile radiated outward to encapsulate Keri in its luminosity. "That's the beauty of life here compared to the earthly plane. There is no time or space in eternity. I'm as close to you as your next breath. All you have to do is believe.

"Close your eyes, suspend your doubts, fears and skepticism and *feel* me with you. Then and only then can you perceive me. It's the same with the angels. They are as real as I and are assigned to protect you in your physical life. But they can not usurp free will. So, unless asked, they stand by, waiting to fulfill God's commands. Every thought has power to affect your actions, Keri. Take care that each one is formed with love and kindness. These are the truths you are to return with and share with others.

"You'll be tempted to forget or to write off this incident as a hallucination brought on by your body's illness and the treatments used to make it viable again. But know this, Keri—God has healed you and made you whole. He gives life, and He does so with unconditional love. Accept His gift and work so that His love and mercy shines through you."

They embraced once more. "Go now, you must start your voyage back."

A bridge made of stone inset with silver and gold, appeared over the water. They walked to the bank and Blossom bent down and pulled something from the riverbed. She placed the smooth, lustrous nugget in Keri's hand. "Keep this always as a remembrance of what you learned and experienced here. Know you are loved beyond measure and that all things are possible to those who believe...in love, in life, in God, in Jesus, in *truth*, and in heaven."

Keri's Christmas Wish

* * * * *

A sense of hope and excitement bubbled through Jeremy as he prepared to go to the hospital Saturday morning. It'd been a week since they'd brought Keri in, but the last couple of days he'd not entertained fear. Instead, confidence buoyed his spirit—and a strong sense that it was only a matter of time before she woke up.

Despite the lack of optimism, the doctors and nurses exhibited, he *knew* things were about to turn around. His mother felt the same. A life coach and spiritual mentor as well as an EM practitioner, Sunni spent hours in prayer and meditation when she wasn't working with clients. She sought wisdom and direction and visualized Keri surrounded by light while the cleansing Blood of Jesus flowed through her body, rendering her healed and whole.

Along with the Jacksons and their prayer partners throughout the community and around the world, they'd formed a veritable fortress of prayers, positive thoughts, and healing energy around Keri.

He arrived at the hospital to find his mother and Mattie massaging Keri's arms and legs to help release toxins from her lymphatic system.

"She feels much cooler today," Mattie observed.

Sunni nodded. "And not as flushed or swollen."

Jeremy kissed each of them on the cheek, then moved to the head of Keri's bed. He leaned down and pressed his lips to her forehead. "She does look and feel better."

The doctor came into the room and the look of relief in his expression lightened the entire atmosphere. "Well, her temperature is normal and has been for nearly twenty-four hours. The infection seems to have subsided substantially. I'm not sure what condition she'll be in if she wakes up, but I think she is somehow, miraculously, out of the woods."

Relief nearly weakened his knees. Jeremy leaned closer and whispered in Keri's ear. "You hear that, sweetheart? You're going to be just fine. C'mon back to us now."

He'd kept the peridot necklace in his shirt pocket for two days. Now he placed it in her palm and closed her fingers around it. He drew back, startled at first when her hand twitched. Then, thrilled, he glanced at the others and found equally stunned expressions on their faces.

"Keep talking to her," the doctor advised.

Jeremy stroked the hair off her face and urged Keri to wake up. "C'mon, sweetheart, open those gorgeous blue eyes, I need to see 'em."

The monitor began to beep as her heart rate accelerated. Her eyelids twitched, then blinked, then opened.

"That's my girl!" Jeremy bent closer. "Can you hear me, Keri? See me?"

Keri nodded, and a weak smile curved her lips. "Hi."

A cheer went up at the sound of her voice.

Jeremy touched his forehead to hers. "Welcome back."

Mattie moved into Keri's view. Tears streamed down her cheeks. "Oh, honey! It's so good to hear your voice. I'm going to go call your dad."

Keri nodded.

"We'd like to run a couple more tests." The doctor's gaze swept the room, then he hurried away.

"What happened?" Keri's gaze held Jeremy's.

"You contracted some kind of rare infection. Had us pretty worried there for a bit."

"How long have I been here?"

"A week."

Sunni stepped close to Jeremy and into Keri's view. He put his arm around his mother and introduced her to the woman he loved.

Keri smiled, then shifted, wanting to shake Sunni's hand. When she opened her fingers, a stone necklace lay nestled against her palm. She looked at it for long moments then closed her fist and placed it against her breast. "It wasn't a dream."

"Keri?"

Jeremy sounded concerned. A kaleidoscope of emotions filled her heart. She closed her eyes a moment, drew in a deep breath then looked up at him. "So much happened while I was away."

Before he could ask questions, two nurses came in to take Keri for the additional tests the doctor had ordered.

"What have we got here?" One nurse patted Keri's closed fist.

She opened her hand to reveal what she held.

"Beautiful, but you can't take it with you."

"I can't be without it."

"I'm sorry, honey, but it's just the way it is. Maybe your young man or his mom can hold it for you until you return."

Keri held the necklace toward Jeremy. "Please don't let anything happen to this."

"We'll both be right here when you get back. I promise. How long will she be gone?"

"A couple of hours, minimum." The nurse busied herself helping Keri onto a gurney.

Doug arrived in time to kiss his daughter before they wheeled her off.

The women chatted while Jeremy and Doug paced. Two and a half hours later, the doctor entered the waiting room, pure bewilderment written on his face.

"I have no idea how to explain what happened or how she pulled through an illness that is normally incurable and often fatal, but Keri is not only out of the woods, her brain seems to be miraculously intact. She'll be weak and I'd like to keep her a couple more days for observation, but unless she relapses or develops further complications, she should be home within a day or two."

Everyone laughed and cried and hugged at the same time. Doug excused himself from the group to call their extended families and church members. Mattie asked when Keri would be back in her room.

"We're moving her from the ICU step down unit into a private room on the next floor up. You can gather your things from here and I'll let you know when she's settled in."

Jeremy, Sunni, and Mattie retrieved the items they'd brought in. Doug rejoined them just as they were summoned to Keri's new room. They found her sitting up while a nursing assistant spoon-fed her a bowl of soup.

She smiled over her liquid meal, then her gaze met Jeremy's. He greeted her with a wink and nod.

The aide filled her water pitcher and picked up the tray. "Can I get anything else for you?"

Keri shook her head. "No, thank you. I'm going to rest a while."

When the young assistant left the room, Keri reached both hands toward her parents. The three conversed in soft hugs and low voices.

"Would you bring some pajamas, Mom? I'd love a nice, hot shower."

Mattie smiled and brushed Keri's hair off her cheeks. "Your father and I will go get some right now. Anything else?"

"Yes...please bring my prayer journal too. It should be by my big chair in the living room."

"You've got it, sweetheart. We'll see you in a little while."

They left and a few minutes later Sunni did also.

Jeremy pulled a chair close to the bed. He took the necklace out of his shirt pocket and placed the chain around her neck, making sure the clasp caught securely.

"It's beautiful." Keri's eyes shimmered.

He brushed his lips across hers. "So good to have you back."

She snuggled deeper into the bedding. "Good to be back," she mumbled. Then she drifted to sleep.

Chapter Ten

When Keri awakened, the sun no longer shone in her hospital room window. She glanced around, noting the drabness of her surroundings. Plain, bland, pristine. No color, only dull gray and white. Tears sprang to her eyes, clogged her airways. She touched the stone at her throat, wrapped her fingers around the pendant and focused on Blossom until her sister appeared in her mind's eye. Tiny pinpricks of awareness tingled through her. Bumps rose on her skin.

"It's so ugly here. I miss you. I miss the beauty and tranquility of Heaven."

Blossom smiled. "That's normal, Keri. Give yourself a chance to get used to life there again."

"But it'll never be the same. *I'm* not the same."

"And you shouldn't be. But you have things to do. Your destiny awaits."

"I don't want to forget. How do I not forget?"

"The power to remember is within you."

"How will I know what my destiny is, or when I've found it?"

"Wisdom and knowledge are yours. Ask and it shall be given unto you."

Keri sniffled. "OK. I love you."

"I love you, too," Blossom whispered as she drifted away.

The door opened. Keri turned over as Jeremy entered.

"Hey, hope I didn't wake you."

She shook her head.

"I just went to grab a bite to eat. Are you hungry?"

Again, Keri replied no with a shake of her head.

He drew close, brushed his lips across her cheek. "Did the cat get your tongue while I was away?"

She smiled and nodded.

Jeremy chuckled as he pulled his chair closer to the bed.

"Feel like talking, or would you prefer to rest?"

"I'd prefer to get out of this bed and into a nice long, hot shower."

"I think that can be arranged." He rang for the nurse, and relayed Keri's request into the intercom.

Moments later a nurse and aide arrived with a wheelchair. They helped Keri into it and pushed her into the bathroom. She emerged refreshed yet exhausted from the simple task of showering.

Still, she shook her head when the two women wheeled her next to the bed. "I'd like to sit up a while."

Jeremy vacated his chair and they transferred her into it.

"Call us when you're ready to get back in bed."

Keri thanked them as they exited the room.

"Feel better?" Jeremy's warm gaze searched her face.

She smiled. "Much."

"There's something I'm dying to know."

She arched a brow.

"When you woke up and saw the necklace in your hand, you said, 'It wasn't a dream.' What did you mean?"

She closed her eyes and took a deep breath as emotion swirled through her remembering the moment Blossom put the nugget in her hand. Every nuance of that eternal moment was etched into her soul. "My sister gave it to me."

She frowned. "I mean.... she gave me the stone. How it became a necklace is beyond me."

Jeremy's gaze reflected awe and wonder—and a thousand questions.

"I have so much I want to tell you but...I'm afraid. What if saying it aloud diminishes the beauty and magic of it all?"

"Maybe you should write everything down first with as much detail as you can remember."

She breathed a sigh. He understood. Jeremy wouldn't pry. "That's a great idea."

He rose and retrieved her journal from the drawer where Mattie had placed it earlier that evening. The moment he held the book within her reach, Keri clasped it with one hand and her necklace with the other as her destiny played out in vivid detail in her mind.

She removed the pen from where it hung on the book's binding and opened to a fresh page. Despite the tremble of her hand when she placed the ball point to paper, words poured forth with stunning clarity.

At last, her eyes could no longer focus, and her fingers cramped. She closed the journal and reattached the pen in its spiral cocoon. "I'm ready to sleep again."

"May I help you, or should we call the nurse?"

She reached a hand toward him. Jeremy smoothed the sheets, then swung Keri up into his arms. He laid her on the bed so gently she almost didn't feel the transition. Something in his gaze stole her breath. Concern. Tenderness. Something else, as well...something she dared not attempt to comprehend.

She snuggled deep into the mattress.

"Should I put that away for you?"

She clutched the journal against her chest. "I don't want anyone to read it until I'm finished."

"OK...."

"I want to remember and record the experience in its entirety without questions or explanations to interrupt the memories."

"Makes sense, but should you really sleep with it?"

His teasing tone forced her to relax, and she smiled. "You can put it away after I fall asleep. I know you won't dishonor my wishes."

He brushed the hair off her cheeks, touched his lips there for a brief caress. "Thank you for that. Your trust and faith mean the world to me."

"Oh, by the way, I met your father. You look a lot like him." She drifted off to sleep with the smile still on her lips.

* * * * *

Keri dreamt. More than a vision of the night, this was a sojourn to another realm. Blossom accompanied her as she saw—

more...she *experienced* beautiful, wondrous scenes of past, present, and future. The moment she awoke, alone in her room, she reached for the journal. Once again, words flowed onto the pages. Rich detail, exotic prose, vivid imagery. True accounts of what she'd seen, heard and experienced while infection raged through her system and her body lay in wait.

When her breakfast arrived, she laid the journal aside and reached for her tray. How could she be so hungry and not have noticed until the aroma of bacon and eggs teased her nostrils? Keri wasted no time enjoying her first real meal since she'd awakened from her week-long nap.

She'd barely finished when her parents strolled in. Mattie walked around the bed to hug her while Doug bent to kiss her cheek.

"When can I get out of here?"

"The doctor should be making rounds in a while. We'll have to ask him." Her mother took the chair Jeremy had left beside the bed and reached for Keri's hand.

"How are you feeling, honey?" This from her dad.

"Fine. I'm ready to be home."

"Well, they'll have to make sure you're able to function on your own before you get to leave. I'm guessing they'll have you up and about some today to see how your motor skills and all that are faring."

As if her father's words had called her forth, a nursing assistant called out a cheery good morning as she came through the door. "Keri, we'll be taking you to physical therapy for evaluation this morning." She glanced at the wall clock. "Actually, within the hour."

"Will we be able to speak with her doctor soon?"

"Yes, ma'am. He'll be here this morning, but later...sometime after Keri's therapy session."

She tidied the tray table and smiled as she left the room.

"Have you heard from Jeremy this morning?" Keri's mother perched on the edge of her chair.

Keri shook her head. "I imagine he'll be here after church." Before her mother could ask the question Keri was sure bounced around her brain, she supplied more information. "He attends a non-denominational church downtown. I've gone with him a time or two and the service is wonderful."

"Good to know." Her dad pinched his chin between thumb and index finger. "We were a bit concerned what his religious orientations were."

Keri laughed. "Jeremy reveres and worships God with his whole heart. He's studied the lives of saints and Christian mystics and believes there is so much more to faith than what the average person considers or exhibits."

She smiled at the skepticism in her father's eyes. "Don't worry, Dad. Really. He's as genuine as they come."

Mattie smiled. "He's a lot like his mother. Sunni is a lovely, fascinating individual."

"I can't wait to get to know her," Keri admitted.

A knock on the door interrupted their conversation. A phlebotomist entered with a smile and a firm hold on his handy blood-drawing paraphernalia. Then an orderly showed up with a wheelchair to take Keri down to PT. He informed them she'd be gone at least an hour or two. "Housekeeping will clean the room while she's gone."

Keri slid her diary into a drawer in her bedside table, breathing a quick, silent prayer of protection over the little book, and then allowed them to help her into the chair. As she transferred from the bed, the necklace she wore swung into view.

"How beautiful," her mother exclaimed. "Where on earth did you get that, Keri...and when? I haven't seen it before."

Keri's heart pounded. What should she say?

"I gave it to her last night." Jeremy answered from the doorway as he and Sunni walked into the room.

Keri released her held breath. "Will you wait here until I return?"

"Of course." He nodded and gave her a slow wink.

"Good." Should anyone be overly curious about what she'd written in her journal, Jeremy would protect her privacy.

"We need to get going." The orderly turned Keri's chair toward the door.

As she rolled away, Keri heard her four visitors discussing breakfast.

Two hours later, exhausted from the battery of tests, Keri slumped in her chair as a different orderly wheeled her back into the room.

"I'd like to sit up for awhile." She allowed him to help her into the chair her father vacated.

Another hour passed before the doctor arrived.

"What's the verdict?" Her father didn't even give the man a chance to say hello.

The doctor's gaze traveled the room—Keri in the chair, Jeremy stretched out on the bed, and all five anxious gazes on him. He chuckled. "The verdict is, other than being weak and somewhat emaciated, our patient here is in excellent condition."

"So, I can go home soon?"

"As I suspected, you'll need a bit of physical therapy. I'd like to keep you another day or two to be certain your improvement is normal and steady, and to be double sure the infection is completely gone. I'll see you again in the morning, and if all is as it should be, we'll talk about when you can go home. After you're discharged, I'd rather you not be alone for at least a week, maybe more. PT will continue until we're positive you're fully capable of managing on your own again."

"We'll make sure she's not alone." Sunni smiled and patted Keri's shoulder.

"OK then. Keri, until I see you tomorrow, I suggest you eat whatever you'd like and as much as you can, walk as often as you want—with an escort, of course—and rest when you're tired. Don't push it."

"I will. Thank you."

He smiled. "You're quite welcome. You, young lady, have restored the faith of many in this field. Everything about your case is unusual, miraculous even, and it's been my pleasure to treat you."

Keri smiled and reached a hand toward him. When he enfolded it in both of his, she gazed into his eyes and allowed the words burning in her heart to flow forth. "The glory goes to God. I know many in your profession don't believe in Him the way those outside of your sphere of colleagues do. But there *is* a God and a purpose for every living creature. Mine may be a rare case, but the evidence is proof, for you and for many to open your mind, heart and soul to believe, in miracles and in Him."

"Thank you, Keri." The doctor squeezed her hand and left the room.

Suddenly weary, Keri asked her father and Jeremy to help her back into bed.

"We'll let you rest now, honey." Her mother tucked the covers around her.

"Thanks, mom. I'll see you and dad later. Or in the morning."

With kisses and murmured goodbyes, her parents left. Sunni followed not long after, but Jeremy stayed and kept watch over her.

* * * * *

While Keri slept, Jeremy immersed himself in deep prayer and meditation. As much as he respected Keri's privacy and the trust and faith she put in him, he wanted to *know* what she'd experienced. He wanted to read her words, hear her voice, and ask the barrage of questions at war within his heart and mind. Like a snarling wolf, impatience in a degree he'd never experienced tugged at every promise he'd made to himself, to Keri and to God.

So, he prayed until the beast slunk away, defeated.

When she awoke, he helped her walk down the hall and back. After helping her get settled in her room again, he made a trip to the local fast food restaurant for lunch. All the while, he struggled with the internal demons of haste and eagerness.

He entered her room and handed her the ham sandwich she'd ordered, then sat in the chair to enjoy his own. Keri took about three bites, then laid her lunch aside.

"Full already?"

"Yeah. Guess my stomach shrunk or something over the last several days."

"That's possible. The sandwich will keep a while so if you're hungry later, you'll have something to nibble on."

She smiled and nodded.

"How's the journaling coming along?"

"Great. I'll need another one before long."

Jeremy smiled. "I'll bring you a fresh one tomorrow. Unless, of course, you think you'll need it tonight?"

She shook her head. "Tomorrow should be fine. I'll need to call my boss tomorrow too. I hope someone contacted the office when all this started."

"Your mom and dad took care of that."

"Good. Thank you so much for being here. How are things going for you?"

Over the next hour or so, without revealing names or identifying details, Jeremy told her some of what had transpired with his clients, especially Jennah Anderson. He kept her talking, even during another trek down the hall and back. Maybe she would reveal at least a little of what she'd experienced.

But Keri said nothing at all about her time out of body. Jeremy bit back his disappointment and when her parents arrived later in the evening, he went home, keeping a tight rein on his impatience and overwhelming curiosity.

Chapter Eleven

On Wednesday, exactly eleven days after being admitted to the hospital, Keri, with her parents' help, traversed the steps into the house where she'd grown up.

"Oh, it is so good to be home." Her voice wobbled.

"You don't know how relieved we are to have you here." Her father hugged her and kissed her cheek.

"Honey, so many people are eager to see you. I'm sure they'll drop by regularly and probably unannounced, so you just tell us when you're tired or want to be alone, and we'll make sure you get the rest you need."

Her mom's voice held a familiar no-nonsense tone. "You'll be busy the next couple of weeks with rehabilitation and so forth, too. So, it's important you stay rested."

"Yeah, I'm so grateful my short term disability with the company has kicked in. That'll come in handy with me missing so much work."

"You don't worry about any of that. If you need a little financial assistance while you get back on your feet, dad and I will be glad to help out."

"Thanks, Mom."

"Now, would you rather lie here on the couch a while or go to your room?"

As much as she appreciated everything her parents had done and were doing, Keri wanted to be alone. "My room, please."

They escorted her into the room she'd occupied for the first eighteen years of her life. A photo of her and Spark brought stinging tears to her eyes. The picture had sat on the bedside table since the day her father took it. After her parents had tucked her in, propped the pillows up behind her, and left her alone,

Keri picked up the framed image and gazed at the beloved animal.

She closed her eyes, but they sprang open in distress. "Mom. MOM!"

Her mother rushed into the room. "What is it?"

"My journals. Please tell me we didn't forget them."

"My goodness, you frightened me half to death!"

"I'm sorry."

Mattie dug through the bag containing Keri's clothing and other personal things and handed the books to her.

"Thanks, Mom," she breathed. "I'm sorry I scared you."

Mattie hugged her close. "It's OK, honey. Is there anything else you need before I go back to the kitchen?"

"No. Thanks."

She clutched her diaries and the portrait against her chest, turned on her side and fell asleep.

The next day began what would become her routine for a couple of weeks. She'd rise and have breakfast with her folks before her father went to work. Her mother would bring her to the outpatient clinic where she did the exercises prescribed by her doctors to regain her former strength and agility.

About the fifth day into her schedule, Jeremy arrived at her parents' home in time for dinner.

"If you feel up to it, I thought maybe we'd go for a drive later." He hiked an eyebrow, his gaze hopeful.

"That would be lovely. Although I go out daily for therapy, I'm starting to get cabin fever."

Jeremy chuckled. "I can imagine."

"Where do y'all plan on going?" her father asked.

Jeremy shrugged. "I'm not sure. We could visit my mom, or maybe take a walk in the park...or just drive along the river or something. I promise not to keep her out too late or tax her energy more than she can handle."

After they'd eaten, Jeremy helped Mattie clear the table while Keri put on shoes and socks for their outing. He escorted her to the car and stood close while she climbed into the vehicle. As he backed out of the drive, he asked if she'd like to go anywhere special.

"Not really. Just getting out of the house for something other than a trip to the outpatient clinic is wonderful." She hesitated a moment then touched his arm. "On second thought, I'd love to go to my apartment. As much as I appreciate staying with my parents, I miss being home."

"I'm sure you do."

They drove the short distance in companionable silence. Once in the apartment, Keri settled in her chair with an audible sigh.

"Can I get you anything? Tea, coffee, water? A snack?"

Keri shook her head and smiled.

He pulled the ottoman close and propped her feet on it, then sat on the couch. "How's the writing coming along?"

"I've nearly filled the second journal you brought me, but I'm pretty sure I got everything down. Once I'm moved back here— soon, I hope—I'd like to re-read it and see if I remember anything else."

Jeremy nodded, his gaze lit with interest. "Sounds like a good idea."

"What about you? You start on any of those books you've talked about writing?"

"Actually, I have. You tell me about yours and I'll tell you about mine." He grinned.

Keri laughed at the teasing light in his eyes and tone of voice. "You'll be the first, if not the only person to read it when I'm done."

Jeremy groaned. "The suspense is eating me alive."

She giggled.

He took her hand then brought it to his lips. "I love that sound."

She arched an eyebrow at him.

"Your laugh fills me with indescribable joy."

Tiny bursts of heat warmed Keri's cheeks when he moved from the couch to kneel beside her.

"I know this might seem sudden, Keri, but nearly losing you made me realize how much you mean to me. Once you get totally on your feet, I'd like for us to talk about a future together."

Keri placed her palm against his cheek. "I'd like that too."

Jeremy lowered his lips to hers in a tender embrace, only to pull away moments later, and sit back on his heels.

Keri's heart beat in a slow, thick thud. Her hands trembled with the need to draw him back into her arms and taste his lips once more. She refrained, afraid of rushing their relationship or putting a strain on her physical strength. That one kiss had weakened her considerably. Jeremy's expression revealed such incredible depth of feeling that tremors shivered through her entire being.

They gazed at each other for a long, lingering moment then Jeremy shifted, rose and returned to his place on the couch. "You said something in the hospital about meeting my dad. Can you tell me about that? I do understand if you'd rather not."

Keri took a deep breath, said a silent prayer, and waited for a sign from the Holy Spirit that it would be OK to share the incident.

When she felt no resistance to the idea, she allowed her eyelids to drift shut and remembered the moment with vivid clarity.

"I'm sure you've guessed that while my body lay ill, my soul traveled to Heaven."

When he didn't answer or even fidget, she continued. "My sister met me almost immediately upon my arrival and explained what was going on. She then said there were others who wanted to greet me. Your father was with my relatives who've passed over from this life into the next. You resemble him quite a bit and although we didn't talk much, I know he loves you and watches over you and your mom."

"You keep mentioning your sister. I didn't know you had a sister, or any other siblings for that matter."

"My mom miscarried the year before she conceived me. But Blossom came to me before, while I was meditating. I wrote everything in

173

my journal then."

"When was that?"

Keri shrugged. "A couple of weeks before the illness I think. I'd have to look back at the date. I didn't tell you about it?"

"No." Jeremy thought back a moment. "But then, if I remember correctly the week or so before your illness was pretty stressful for both of us."

"True. I'll show you when we get back to Mom and Dad's."

When she began to tire, Jeremy drove them back to her parents' house. As they started upstairs, her father came out from the living room.

"Where are you two going?"

"Up to my room."

Her father's sharp inhale reached her ears, and Keri turned to him before he could speak. "I'll leave the door open, Daddy. I just want to show Jeremy something. I promise he won't be long."

Jeremy hesitated until Doug nodded his acquiescence.

"Sorry, he's a little old fashioned." Keri kept her voice quiet.

Jeremy grinned. "That's OK. I'm sure I'll be that way too when I have a daughter."

The intimate quality of his voice sent shivers down her spine. Keri waved him into the chair by her desk then walked around the bed to retrieve her journal out of the nightstand drawer.

She picked up the book, turned to the entry and held it toward Jeremy. "You can read it, but please don't read further. I'd really like to keep everything that happened while I was ill private until it is completely recorded. As I said earlier, I'm pretty sure it's finished but I'd like to be assured of that before I let anyone read it."

Keri took Jeremy's nod to be both understanding and promise. When he reached for it with hands that trembled, she released her hold on the journal. When he closed the book, his eyes glazed with astonishment, she took it back and held it close to her heart.

"Wow."

The wonder in his voice echoed what stirred in her soul. She still couldn't believe the gift she'd been given or the assignment that now rested on her shoulders.

She had to tell her story to all. She had to share the truth of everything she learned and experienced while on her journey to the Promised Land.

* * * * *

The next few weeks passed as if on wings. Keri's doctors proclaimed her progress miraculous. She returned to work part time until she felt healthy enough to go back to her regular schedule. Within a month her recovery was complete and her life back on track.

Only she was different in so many ways.

The frustration she'd often felt toward circumstances and people was replaced with love, appreciation, and compassion. She remembered Blossom's edict on how powerful thoughts were and took great care to fill her mind with words and images of love, peace, joy, happiness, forgiveness, grace, mercy, kindness—every good thing imaginable.

She spent hours each morning and evening and moments throughout the day replenishing her depleted energy with quiet meditation. She also learned to gauge a person's interest and intent when asked about her time in the hospital and responded accordingly, careful to reveal only what the Holy Spirit allowed for the edification of whom she talked with.

When at last she knew her recollection of her time in heaven and all that transpired was complete, she allowed Jeremy to read what she'd written. He did so in nightly increments, when he visited each evening as summer dwindled into early fall.

* * * * *

Jeremy closed the journal after he'd read the final entry–Keri's account of the journey back into her earthly body.

"This needs to be published, Keri. People all over the world need to read what you've written. They need to know the truth of God and Heaven."

"I've thought the same thing. I'm only waiting for God to reveal to me the perfect time and publisher to approach."

"That's a good idea. I have a friend from college who is always after me to complete the books I've talked about and send them to him. Would you want me to contact him?"

"Who is he with?"

Keri's eyes widened in surprised shock when he named the same publishing company she'd felt in her spirit would accept her book. "Yes, please contact him."

Two weeks later, Keri gazed out a café window, awed and humbled at the beauty of the holiday decorations which lined the streets and every doorway in New York. She breathed in the scent of cinnamon and vanilla that perfumed the air. She and Jeremy sat with his friend while the gentleman, Chip, read her journals.

He had flown in from California to visit with a couple of authors he'd contracted and wanted to see if her story fit the editorial needs of his company. He closed the book and cleared his throat before speaking.

"We'd love to have this. Do you want to type it up or should I take these and have that done for you?"

"Oh, no, I'll type it myself. That way if anything comes to mind that I didn't remember before, I can include it in the final version."

"Great idea. How soon can you get it to me?"

She shrugged. "How soon do you need it?"

"As soon as humanly possible." He laughed. "I believe we can put a rush on it and get this into our lineup for publication next year."

He swiped the screen on his tablet, asked for Keri's email address and tapped it into his contact program. "My assistant will email a contract to you within the week. Do you think I could have the typed version by Christmas?"

"Yes, that's completely doable."

"Wonderful." He rose from his chair. "This will be an amazing book, Keri, and will probably set your life on a whole new course. Are you ready for that?"

Keri glanced out the window as snow began to fall, turning the evening into a shimmering globe of light and color. "I'm ready for whatever God wills."

"Great. We'll meet back here on the twentieth of December. If you can't complete the task by then, just let me know and we'll push the meeting back a little but no later than the end of this year. We'll need several months to get through the pre-publication process of editing, cover design, marketing, etcetera."

Keri rose when Jeremy did and the three of them shook hands.

"Thank you for allowing me to read your incredible journey, Keri." Chip glowered at Jeremy. "You're next, so get busy on that book we've outlined."

They laughed and parted ways.

New York was alive and in full swing of the holiday season when they met again on the twentieth of December. Keri gazed out the hotel window while Jeremy and Chip sat at the table in the penthouse suite. Her heart hammered in anticipation. She heard his exclamation of delight and turned to see the expression on his and Jeremy's faces as they closed the binder after reading the last page of her manuscript.

"I love the way you ended this! And I'm glad you didn't let me read it until now." Jeremy chuckled, and Keri grinned at his droll expression.

Chip nodded in agreement. "Yes, a perfect ending."

He picked up the binder, opened to the final page, and read...

"My Christmas wish was granted in a way only God could have orchestrated. As Blossom, Spark and I flew over the various manger

scenes laid out below during every season imaginable, I learned something profound. When Jesus was born doesn't matter, only the fact that He was, He is, and He ever shall be... in a world without end. Amen.

Dear Readers,

If you've followed me throughout the years of my writing career, I thank you from the bottom of my heart.

If you're a new reader, welcome to my world!

Like Keri, many folks (myself included) get fed up with the hype and commercialism of Christmas, so much so that we forget to recognize and honor the *real* reason for the season..... **Jesus.**

In fact, He is the reason for every season. With this in mind, on the following pages, I'm sharing a few Christmas poems I've written throughout the years. I sincerely hope you enjoy them.

If you don't already know Him, I pray you will pursue a relationship with the Lord Jesus. If you do, call upon Him in your time of trouble, for He will hear and answer. As always, may God bless and keep you −and yours− in the palm of His mighty hand!

Pamela S Thibodeaux
"Inspirational with an Edge!" ™

Christmas Wish

As I wish upon a star,
in the silent night above.

I'm reminded of the holy night,
God sent His gift of love.

A precious Child to light our way,
with hope & promise of a better day.

Wrapped in swaddling, asleep in the hay,
the King of Kings to whom we now pray.

My wish for you this Christmas Day,
is that blessings & favor prepare your way.

And peace, joy, goodwill & cheer,
fill your heart each day of the year.

From My Heart to Yours

In this season of giving and good cheer, I've a message for all to hear!

Good news and glad tidings sent to all men, for a Savior was born in the town of Bethlehem.

Christ the Lord came down to earth, born in a manger, from holy to lowly by birth.

Throughout His life He chose to live right, to be an example of God's power and might.

To die on a cross in just a few years, but never FEAR!

For in victory He rose from that awful grave.

To give Life to all those He came to save.

So, in this time of giving and season of cheer...Remember, Christ is to be praised all through the year.

The Blessing of Family

As wise men once followed a bright, shining
star
We gather together from near and from far.

A special bonding of hearts, of life and of blood
A sign, a wonder! A miracle from above.

Though our lives are far apart,
We come together; one Spirit, one Heart.

We gather to celebrate the blessed day
When Jesus was born to light our way.

We gather as a family in joy and in love
To honor God's perfect gift from above.

From our hearts to yours...May the
Blessings and miracles of this Holy Season be
yours throughout the years to come.

The Blessing of Friends
Prov. 18:24

We've heard it all before, but I'll say it again,
there's no greater blessing than that of a friend.

Dearer to us than a sister or a mother, God
defines a friend as one closer than a brother.

Being a true friend, doesn't take much

A shoulder, an ear, a special touch.

You've been all of this to us and so much more,
you're someone we love, cherish, and adore.

God came to earth on the wings of a dove, to be
a friend to man and to show us His love.

A true friend is One who will lay down His life,
Christ was born for this purpose, the perfect
Sacrifice.

As we count our blessings this Holiday Season,
we know God placed you in our lives for this
reason.

The Gift

No gift ever given, great or small
can compare to greatest Treasure of all.

Born in a manger in the town of Bethlehem
Christ the Lord, who died for all men.

Sometimes referred to as the 'Pearl of Great
Price'
God so loved the world that He sent His Son to
die
–the perfect sacrifice.

So please remember in this season of cheer
God is to be honored and praised
each day of the year.

About the Author

Pamela S. Thibodeaux grew up in the town of Iowa, Louisiana. She is the mother of four (two by blood and two by marriage) and a grandmother. A deeply committed Christian, Pamela firmly believes in God and His promises.

"God is very real to me, and I feel people today need and want to hear more of His truths wherever they can glean them. People are hungry for practical (and real) Christian values, not some 'holier-than-thou' beliefs which are impossible to believe and impossible to live up to," Pamela says.

"I do my best to encourage readers to develop a personal relationship with God. The deepest desire of my heart is to glorify God and to get His message of faith, trust, and forgiveness to a hurting world."

Email Pamela at:
pam@pamelathibodeaux.com

Visit her website:
http://www.pamelathibodeaux.com

Or blog:
http://pamswildroseblog.blogspot.com

Sign up to Receive Pam's Newsletter and get a FREE short story!

Also: be sure to follow Pam on Social Media: FaceBook, Twitter @psthib, Amazon Author Page, Instagram, Pinterest, GoodReads, and BookBub.

Other Titles by Pamela S Thibodeaux

Love's Overcoming Power

Temptation, Abuse, Grief and Doubt are plagues common to women all over the world. In John, 16 Jesus said.... In the world you will have tribulation but be of good cheer, for I have overcome the world.

In this Women's Fiction collection comprised of three full-length novels and one novella, Pamela S Thibodeaux shares stories that exemplify the power of God's love to overcome whatever situations life throws at you.

Includes: *The Visionary, Circles of Fate, My Heart Weeps* and *Keri's Christmas Wish.*

My Heart Weeps

When life takes everything, your world stops. Can a retreat heal the broken lives of two wounded souls?

Melena Rhyker's world shattered the day her husband died. Lost without the man of her dreams, she digs deep to find a path out of her sorrow. Discovering an artistic retreat, she vows to find a reason to carry on and focus her life in a new direction. Can she heal her own heart, and find her new beginning?

Garrett Saunders knows pain. He's spent most of his life hiding from his past. Regrets and lies haunt him, but he longs to leave them behind and embrace his true self. Will Melena's efforts to rebuild her life in the face of such grief encourage him to exorcise his own demons of guilt and shame?

Will two hurting people find peace, wholeness and perhaps love in the heart of Texas?

Get this second chance women's fiction novel today and see how love and faith conquers all.

Circles of Fate

Set at the tail end of the Vietnam War era, **Circles of Fate** takes the reader from Fort Benning, Georgia to Thibodaux, Louisiana. A romantic saga, this gripping novel covers nearly twenty years in the lives of Shaunna Chatman and Todd Jameson. Constantly thrown together and torn apart by fate, the two are repeatedly forced to choose between love and duty, right and wrong, standing on faith or succumbing to the world's viewpoint on life, love, marriage and fidelity. With intriguing twists and turns, fate brings together a cast of characters whose lives will forever be entwined. Through it all is the hand of God as He works all things together for the good of those who love Him and are called according to His purpose.

The Visionary ~ Will the ugly secret haunting the twins keep them from finding true love?

While most visionaries see into the future, Taylor sees the past. but only as it pertains to her work. Hailed by her peers as "a visionary with an instinct for beauty and an eye for the unique" Taylor is undoubtedly a brilliant architect and gifted designer. But she and twin brother Trevor, share more than a successful business. The two share a childhood wrought with lies and deceit and the kind of abuse that's disturbingly prevalent in today's society.

Can the love of God and the awesome healing power of His grace and mercy free the twins from their past and open their hearts to the good plan and the future He has for their lives?

Love is a Rose (devotional)

Music is the magical entry into the spirit world; the golden gate into the Kingdom of God. But we mustn't be of the mindset that God only uses Christian music to reach out and touch our mind, heart and spirit. God uses any and every means available to speak to His children.

Our job is to be open and receptive.

In this devotional, Pamela S Thibodeaux shares how God opened her spirit to a deeper understanding of the abundance of His grace and mercy through the words of the song, The Rose sung by Country & Western artist Conway Twitty.

Pamela offers Seeds to Ponder and a prayer as she parallels the love of God and the Christian life to each verse of the song.

The Tempered Series Collection

Start at the beginning and follow these beloved characters throughout the years as love crosses the lines of age and strengthens the bonds of friendship. Contains: **Tempered Hearts, Tempered Dreams, Tempered Fire, Tempered Joy, Lori's Redemption**

Tempered Hearts

Rancher Craig Harris and veterinarian Tamera Collins clash from the moment they meet. Innocence is pitted against arrogance as tempers rise and passions ignite to form a love as pure as the finest gold, fresh from the crucible and as strong as steel. Thrown together amid tragedy and unsated passion, Tamera and Craig share a strong attraction that neither accepts as the first stages of love. Torn between desire and dislike, they must make peace with their pasts and God in order to open up to the love blossoming between them. It is a love that nothing can destroy when they come to understand that *only when hearts are tempered, minds are opened, and wills are softened can man discern the will of God for his life.*

Tempered Dreams

Dr. Scott Hensley (introduced in Tempered Hearts) has built a wall around his heart since the death of his wife and parents. Katrina Simmons is recovering from scars inflicted on her as a battered wife. Can dreams be renewed and faith strengthened? Can they find joy and peace in God's love and in love for one another?

Tempered Fire

Amber Harris is a good girl on the brink of womanhood. Stanley Morrison is a young man at the start of his life. For each other, they have always felt the fireworks that two people in love should feel. However, the questions about his past, his pride, and Amber's father might be the end of what could be a strong relationship. As the two try to protect their budding romance, some unlikely but powerful forces conspire to keep them apart. Will they survive the wishes of everyone around them with their relationship intact?

Tempered Joy

All around rodeo cowboy and heir to the Rockin' H Ranch, Ace Harris is determined not to fall in love. He's only loved one woman in his life, his mother, and no one can even come close to filling her boots. Lexie Morgan thinks rodeo cowboys have rocks for brains and a death wish for a soul. A broken childhood and the death of her father and best friend leave her doubting and questioning God (despite her years of religious upbringing) and afraid of love. Can two young people who clash from the onset learn to trust in the healing power of God and find love and happiness amidst tragedy and grief?

Lori's Redemption (spin-off novella)

Lori Strickland (introduced in *Tempered Fire*) has always been known as her father's "wild child" with no desire to change until she meets ex-bull-rider-turned-preacher Rafe Judson. Her attempts to change her wanton ways come to naught until she realizes redemption only comes with true repentance. Can she find redemption and win the heart of the cowboy preacher?

Tempered Truth (Book 5)

Fate declared them neighbors. Scandal insisted they were brothers. The fact that they looked enough alike to be twins only added fuel to the rumors flying about their parentage.

For fifty-plus years Craig Harris and Scott Hensley have enjoyed a bond nothing can sever.

Not the insinuations that they share the same father.

Not the years of strife and grief and heartache.

Not even death.

Will the truth set them free, or will it destroy the friendship that has lasted a lifetime?

The Inheritance

The Inheritance is about the chance we all long for...the chance to start over. Widowed at age thirty-nine and suffering from empty nest syndrome, Rebecca Sinclair is overshadowed by grief and loneliness. Her husband has been deceased for a year, her oldest child has moved to New York in pursuit of an acting career and her youngest child is attending college in France. Having spent over half of her life as a wife and mother, she has no idea what God has in store for her now. Will an unexpected inheritance in the wine country of New York bring meaning and purpose to her life and give her the courage to love again?

US Postal worker Raymond Jacobey has been in love with the little widow since he first set eyes on her. A wanderer searching for the ever-elusive soul mate, Ray has never stayed in one place too long. Raised by self-centered, high-power executives, he's longed for the idyllic life of residing in a cozy house in a small town with the love of his life. Will he gain the heart of the lovely widow, or will he lose her to the wine country of New York?

Anytime is the perfect time for love.

In *Love in Season,* author Pamela S Thibodeaux brings together eight of her most beloved romance stories—one for each season plus four holidays that revolve around love and family. Includes (Winter) **Winter Madness**, (Valentine's Day) **Choices**, (Spring) **Cathy's Angel**, (Easter) **Lilies for Sandi** (NEW), (Summer) **The Big Catch** (NEW), (Fall) **A Hero for Jessica**, (Thanksgiving) **Review of Love** (NEW) and (Christmas) **In His Sight**

Sienna has survived what most succumb to - the death of a spouse and child and has maintained her faith despite her troubles. William has never met anyone who actually lived out what they say they believe. Is it true love between the faithful optimist and broody pessimist or simply *Winter Madness*? Part of *Love in Season* collection of short stories.

Best-selling novelist and songwriter, Camie Rogers has penned numerous accounts of the secret love she holds in her heart. Country-Music Superstar Kip Allen has changed from the shy, humble boy, to the epitome of "star." Can the two rediscover each other after one night of his Home is Where the Heart is Tour? Find out in **Choices,** Part of **Love in Season** collection of short stories.

Single mom Cathy Johnson is tired of running her life alone...what she needs is a well-trained angel to help out. Jared Savoy gave up the dream of having a family when he discovered he is sterile. Can a confirmed bachelor and the mother of four find love amid normal daily chaos? Find out in **Cathy's Angel** Part of **Love in Season** collection of short stories.

Sandi and Brett did everything backwards. They got pregnant before the wedding and had a baby instead of a honeymoon. Since, Brett has resented the fact that his dreams of a football career have been cut short and wonders how long it'll take God to forgive him for his mistakes. Sandi has played second fiddle to Brett's dreams and desires to the point of not knowing herself any longer and fears her marriage will never be a true one because of their failures. Can two hearts broken by unfulfilled dreams find healing, wholeness, and restoration? Find out in **Lilies for Sandi** Part of **Love in Season** collection of short stories.

Karla and, the love of her life, Jeff, have uncovered some uncommon ground: The Great Outdoors. For the life of her, she does not understand his love of fishing and how he can spend so much time doing so. Will she come to love the sport as much as he or will his passion for a rod and reel tangle up their relationship? Find out in **The Big Catch** Part of **Love in Season** collection of short stories.

Anthony Paul Seville is known as the 'most eligible bachelor' in New Orleans, possibly even the entire state of Louisiana, but finds himself alone—completely and explicitly alone. Jessica Aucoin is a writer on her way to fame and fortune but is haunted by a man from her past. Will the "champion" lawyer and the author of romantic suspense find love written in their future? Find out in **A Hero for Jessica**, Part of **Love in Season** collection of short stories.

Jason Stockwell has been commissioned to interview Kylie Erickson and to review her books. Only problem is, she won't give the time of day much less an interview to someone whose type of writing she deems not worthy of respect. Can they suspend their judgmental attitudes and find true love? Find out in **Review of Love** Part of **Love in Season** collection of short stories.

Grade-school teacher Carson Alexander has a gift—a gift that has driven a wedge between him and his family. Worse, it's put him at odds with God. Feeling alone and misunderstood, Carson views God's gift of prophecy as the worst kind of curse...that is until he meets Lorelei Conner, landscape artist extraordinaire, and perhaps the one person who may need Carson and his gift more than anyone ever has.

Lorelei Connor is a mother on the run. Her abusive ex-husband has followed her all over the country trying to steal their daughter. Distrusting of men and needing to keep on the move, she's surprised by her desire to remain close to Carson Alexander. Through her fear and hesitation, she must learn to rely on God to guide her—not an easy task when He's prompting her to trust a man. Can their relationship withstand the tragedy lurking on the horizon? Find out in **In His Sight,** Part of **Love in Season** collection of short stories.

Once Again,
Thank You.....

I pray you've been blessed as I have by your purchase of this book. If you've enjoyed **Keri's Christmas Wish** please write a positive review and post it at online retailers (Amazon, B&N, Kobo, iBooks, etc.) and websites where readers gather and/or your social media platforms (FaceBook, Good Reads, BookBub, Twitter, etc).

Sign up to receive my **Newsletter** and get a FREE short story.

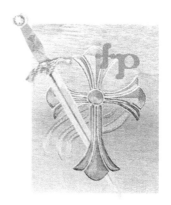

Temperance
Publishing